AND THEN
THERE WAS
NUN

Also by
Monica Quill

NOT A BLESSED THING!

LET US PREY

AND THEN THERE WAS NUN

A
SISTER MARY TERESA
MYSTERY
BY
Monica Quill

THE VANGUARD PRESS
New York

Copyright © 1984 by Monica Quill.

Published by Vanguard Press, Inc.,

424 Madison Avenue, New York, N.Y., 10017.

Published simultaneously in Canada by Book Center, Inc.,

Montreal, Quebec.

Library of Congress Cataloging in Publication Data

McInerny, Ralph M.
    And then there was nun.
    I. Title.
PS3563.A31166A85   1984   813'.54   83-23595
ISBN 0-8149-0879-9

Designer: Tom Bevans

Manufactured in the United States of America

1   2   3   4   5   6   7   8   9   0

For
Alice and Daniel Osberger

AND THEN
THERE WAS
NUN

One

The woman standing on the porch of the house on Walton Street was middle-aged, well-groomed, and nervous. She was also visibly annoyed that Kim did not immediately open the door to her.

"Sister Mary Teresa will remember me. I was a student of hers. Diana Moore. My married name is Torrance, but she wouldn't know that. Is she in?"

Diana Moore Torrance posed a moral dilemma for Kim. On the one hand, Sister Mary Teresa Dempsey did not like to be interrupted during the hours she spent in her study composing her *magnum opus* on the twelfth century, a book aimed at bringing together the vast and varied knowledge the old nun had accumulated in more than half a century of teaching and research. On the other hand, Emtee Dempsey — the acronym with which Kim and Joyce referred to their elderly colleague in the Order of

Martha and Mary—took special pleasure in seeing alumnae of the college the M. & M.s had run west of Chicago for so many years. Five years ago it had been sold off and the nuns moved into a large house on Walton Street designed by Frank Lloyd Wright, intent on pursuing more relevant work. The experiment had decimated their ranks and now only three nuns remained in the once prospering order: Sisters Mary Teresa, Kimberly, and Joyce.

"I must speak with her," Diana Moore Torrance said, pressing close to the screen door as if she wanted to become invisible to hostile forces. The memory of other such callers decided Kim and she opened the door.

The decision turned out to be the right one. Emtee Dempsey, dressed as always in the full anachronistic splendor of the habit designed by the Blessed Abigail Keineswegs, foundress of the Order of Martha and Mary, put down her fountain pen and looked up through rimless spectacles at Kim.

"Of course I'll see her. Show her in, Sister Kimberly."

Their guest seemed surprised that Emtee Dempsey referred to Kim as Sister Kimberly, but did not object when the old nun asked Kim to stay. After Kim had gone to the kitchen for the coffee, that is.

Joyce, wearing jeans and a baggy sweat shirt with a fading "Notre Dame" lettered on it, was frowning over a cookbook. She cupped a cigarette in her hand; the back door was ajar to permit her to get rid of the cigarette quickly at the sound of Emtee Dempsey thumping down the hall on her cane. The old nun and Joyce both promoted the fiction that Joyce's smoking was an undiscovered habit.

"Who was at the door?" Joyce asked.

"An alumna of the college."

Joyce began to hum the school song, running a hand through her short cropped hair. "Emtee will like that. Sometimes even I miss the place."

Sister Mary Teresa had been adamantly opposed to the sale and argued that for the Order to veer from education, its long-standing work, to the social ministry was a massive mistake. She had been proved right and she was not above calling attention to the way events had vindicated her position. The use of the mind was, in the old nun's view, as important a work as any other, and she considered it particularly essential that women be engaged in the intellectual life. She herself had had a great influence on many students, Kim among them. But somehow Kim did not think it was memories of the life of the mind that had brought Diana to their door that morning.

When Kim returned to the study with the coffee, Diana was seated across the desk from the fat little nun, a lighted cigarette in her hand. She nodded when Kim put a cup of coffee at her elbow but went right on talking to Emtee Dempsey.

"Anyway, I've decided to leave him, Sister. I don't expect you to understand that, let alone approve it, but I don't see that there is anything else I can do. We haven't been happy together." Her voice trailed away wistfully and she dragged on her cigarette.

"How long has it been since you graduated, Diana?"

"Twenty years."

"Has it really been that long?"

Did Sister Mary Teresa still see this woman as a student? Kim could see marks of age in the tanned skin, and their visitor's blonde hair was certainly more than an act of God. Diana's light blue cotton dress and navy blue shoes were simple yet expensive-looking. There were no rings on the relevant finger of the small left hand, but the skin was pale where they had recently been.

"And when did you marry Philip Torrance?" Emtee Dempsey asked.

"Three weeks after graduation." There was a wondering note in her voice, as if she were recounting a practical joke.

"Any children?"

"No." She hesitated. "I couldn't have any. I tried every-thing. For years I went to doctors, only to have my hopes raised and then dashed. Finally we just accepted it. I accepted it, any-way. We talked of adoption but Phil just couldn't go through with it."

"And now you want to leave him?"

"He left me, Sister, long ago, in every important sense. Just living together doesn't make a marriage. I have decided to rec-ognize a fact, not create one."

Diana spoke both defensively and assertively. Kim supposed it took courage to say these things to the forbidding little nun. Emtee Dempsey's views on the indissolubility of marriage, the virtue of fidelity, and weathering life's storms could be described as firm or unrealistic, depending on the viewpoint of the one hearing them. Still, Kim was sure the old nun had no intention of lecturing Diana Moore Torrance on the sanctity of the marri-age bond and the significance of the phrase "for better or worse."

"And you wanted to tell me all about it."

For the first time Diana smiled. It was a sadly attractive smile that made her eyes sparkle. But her eyes sparkled only be-cause they were moist.

"Do you know, Sister, for years now I've wanted to come see you? Not to bring you a tale of woe, but just to talk. I still re-member your classes. Everything seemed so clear then."

"Now, you wouldn't have learned from me that the world is a simple place, Diana. Or that life is easy."

"Please don't tell me to tough it out and stay with him. For the last seven years I've been doing exactly that. I've stayed with him only out of a sense of obligation."

"Seven years?"

"That was when I first learned there were other women."

Emtee Dempsey's sigh was eloquent. Diana brought her cup to her lips but her eyes never left the old nun. She seemed hopeful that she would hear something to restore the clear view of life she imagined she had had long ago when she was a student of Sister Mary Teresa's. The smile returned, smaller now.

"When I came here, do you know what I imagined? That you would ask me to stay. Move in with you. Like a retreat or something. It's not that I'm afraid or anything like that. But I could use the solitude."

Did she think Emtee Dempsey would see her hope as anything other than a further attempt to escape from her life? Retreat was the right word, Kim thought, and not in its religious sense.

"Tell me about your husband, Diana."

The sketch, given after a token sip of coffee and a symbolic intake of breath, was surprisingly brief. Phil Torrance had graduated from DePaul two years before Diana received her degree from the College of Martha and Mary. Torrance had been student manager of two varsity teams, basketball and baseball. He was an English major, but sports were his life, vicarious sports. He himself played nothing well. He averaged 120 in golf, his tennis was vigorous but sacrificial, his handball was enough to give a cardiologist pause. After graduation, he took a job at Wrigley Field, on the outer periphery of the Cubs organization. From there he went to the Blackhawks as assistant director of publicity until eight years ago when, with borrowed money, he founded a woman's professional soccer team. Interest in the sport was just beginning to crescendo and Torrance's became an increasingly lucrative franchise.

"Have you ever heard of the team, Sister?"

"Oh, I must have," Emtee Dempsey said vaguely, her eye straying to Kim.

Kim asked, "What are they called?" Of the women in the house, only Joyce would know such things.

"The Brass." Diana made a face. "They're sometimes called the Bras. I suppose we asked for that."

Clearly Diana had been more than a spectator of this endeavor by her husband.

"I am one of the vice presidents," she said with solemn pride. "My responsibility is Personnel. Contracts. Despite my education, I find I am quite a good accountant. I don't travel with the team."

"But your husband does?"

"He has to." The remark might have been the echo of his response in an ancient quarrel. "At least he thinks he has to. Phil is the George Steinbrenner of women's soccer."

Kim and Emtee Dempsey exchanged a look. Kim wondered if Diana realized how little the two of them knew of sports. But it would have been difficult to guess that Sister Mary Teresa had never before heard of the Chicago Brass and was unaware that there was such a phenomenon as women playing soccer for incredible sums of money. The old nun questioned Diana about the organization of the corporation that owned the team, the team's schedule, revenue, salaries. And then the conversation turned to the star of the team, Vivian Hoy.

"I signed her," Diana said. "And she has been worth her weight in gold."

"This woman kicks a ball around a field for a living?" Emtee Dempsey sat forward and laid her fat little hands flat upon her desk.

"She is also very beautiful," Diana said with obvious reluctance. "Beautiful and amoral."

"How long has she been with the team?"

"For five years." She looked steadily at the old nun. "She was not the first of Phil's women, but she is one of them — the most important one."

"One of them?"

"That's right. There are others. But that can be Vivian's problem now. It is not going to be mine anymore."

"Will you continue as vice president if you leave your husband?"

"You bet I will. The Brass is mine as well as his." She smiled bitterly. "I guess that team is the only baby we ever had and I am certainly not going to let Phil have custody of it."

That was the essence of the story Diana Moore Torrance came to tell Emtee Dempsey. But of course she did not stick to the essence, and once the main lines of her sad narrative were laid out, she wanted to embellish them. It was pretty clear to Kim that what Diana really wanted but didn't expect was for the old nun to tell her she was doing exactly the right thing and that nobody, herself and God included, would think less of her for leaving her husband. As she often had before, Emtee Dempsey surprised Kim by the compassion she showed toward a person caught up in one of the social ills the old nun condemned so roundly in the abstract. Maybe she did remember Diana as a girl. She certainly remembered an incredible number of the young women who had taken history from her and, despite her forbidding exterior, had found in her just the confidante they wanted and needed when crises arose. Why else did they come back in such numbers, finding the old nun, even in this unlikely stopping place on Walton, a reassuring symbol in a world that seemed to change with such dizzying rapidity? But if the old nun did not condemn Diana, neither did she encourage her to leave her husband.

Although a good deal of Sister Mary Teresa's morning had been taken up by her caller, it would not have been apparent to Diana how much the loss of those hours meant. The old nun worked in a highly disciplined way, her output was steady and according to schedule, but she professed to hear time's chariot at her heels. She did not propose to leave an unfinished manuscript on her desk if she could avoid it. There are things more important than literary plans, however, and the problem that brought Diana to the door of the house on Walton Street was one of them. When the old nun asked if Diana would like to spend a few days with them, Diana seemed to forget that the idea originated with her.

"Maybe I would. May I call you about it later today?"

"My dear, you may call whenever you like."

Emtee Dempsey accompanied Diana down the hallway to the front door and showed her out. She remained there for a moment, watching her former student hurry into an expensive automobile. There was a pensive look on her face when she returned to the study, and her cane did not make its usual emphatic sound. She picked up her fountain pen, then put it down again. She shook her head.

"That woman was a brilliant student."

"Do you remember her?"

Emtee Dempsey looked sharply at Kim. "I remember all my students."

Diana did not phone Sister Mary Teresa later that day, but if the old nun was surprised she did not show it. Joyce, as expected, proved to be a mine of information on the Chicago Brass. She knew the team's record thus far this season, she explained how it worked its way up from a position of obscurity in the league to a place of contention, and she knew all its players. She had gleaned all this from the sports page, never having attended a game in person. Neither Kim nor Emtee Dempsey had suspected Joyce's interest in soccer, but then, there were few sports Joyce was not interested in. It was a sad thought that her knowledge of them was almost as academic as Sister Mary Teresa's knowledge of the twelfth century, something gleaned from reports and documents rather than from personal experience.

"You must go watch them play," Emtee Dempsey said. She

was sincere, though her voice was strange. She really could not imagine anyone wanting to spend hours watching adult human beings kick a ball back and forth on a field. Of course, playing ball was a medieval phenomenon, or so it was alleged, so the subject almost made it as a topic of importance.

"They're out of town this week," Joyce said. "I don't have to see a game."

"I didn't imagine it was a matter of necessity," Emtee Dempsey said dryly. "What exactly is the principle of soccer, Sister Joyce? What special skills does it require?"

She frowned through Joyce's recital and Kim wondered if any game would not sound ridiculous when explained. Joyce was particularly laudatory of Vivian Hoy, star of the Brass and current high scorer in the league.

"Phil Torrance has done wonders," Joyce said. "All the sports writers say so. Not only for the Brass, but for the whole league. He has done for Chicago women's soccer what George Halas did for the Bears and the NFL."

This remark required interpretation and Joyce was glad to give it.

The conversation took place at lunch on the day Diana Moore Torrance had stopped by the house on Walton Street. Listening to Joyce, Kim reminded herself that the word "fan" is a diminutive of "fanatic." Going to a Chicago Brass contest with Joyce would have been the sisterly thing to do, but Kim was glad there was no game that night. She herself had a number of other things to do, like attending an afternoon seminar at Northwestern, where she was a graduate student in history. Her choice was due to the influence Sister Mary Teresa had had on her as a student. That had been before Kim joined the Order of Martha and Mary.

"Boarding the sinking ship," as Joyce cheerfully put it. Joyce would have been happy enough staying on at the college.

She was happy enough to be in charge of the house on Walton Street. Joyce had a great talent for adapting.

Two days after Diana paid her visit on her old college professor, the body of her husband, Philip Torrance, was found floating face down in Belmont Harbor. Kim heard the news on the car radio when she was on her way for a morning's research at the Northwestern library. She pulled over to the curb and listened with her mouth open. Then she put the car in gear and drove home. When she got back to Walton Street, she ran down the hall and burst into Emtee Dempsey's study. The old nun was behind her desk. Seated across from her was Diana Moore Torrance. The younger woman looked at Kim with widened yet somehow expressionless eyes.

"You've heard about my husband?"

Kim nodded. "Just. It was on the news."

"Oh, my God. What did they say?"

Emtee Dempsey snorted. "Don't worry about what will be said. You know what will be said. Everyone is going to think that you were responsible for his death. Isn't that what you've been telling me? The question is not what will be said but how you can show it is not true."

"How can I show that? Whatever I say will make matters worse."

"Did you kill him?"

"No!"

"But you had what are considered good reasons to. Reasons in the plural. And you had opportunity. Let us review the facts."

The facts were bleak indeed. At eleven o'clock the previous night Diana had picked up her husband at O'Hare when he arrived with the members of the Chicago Brass from a game in St. Louis. The team had scattered to their several destinations — all but Vivian Hoy. At Philip Torrance's suggestion, they had driven her into town and on the way, because of the heat, he had proposed they stop at Belmont Harbor and go out to his anchored boat. For Diana to have objected to this would have led to a quarrel she did not wish to have, particularly in the obtaining circumstances. She regretted not being alone with her husband, but only because she intended to tell him she had decided to leave him.

"Talking with you settled my mind, Sister. He was not likely to change and I was through being humiliated by him."

"I did not advise you to leave him. As a result of your visit, I had made up my mind to have a talk with your husband."

"Why?"

"One does not need to be an historian to know there are two sides to every story."

"What is that supposed to mean?"

"I'll never know. Not now."

"Sister, he would never have admitted what I told you."

Emtee Dempsey straightened in her chair. The great winged headdress she wore, identical to that featured in portraits of the Blessed Abigail Keineswegs, stirred, then settled like a bird upon her head. Her expression suggested that Philip Torrance would have been ill advised to try to mislead her.

"Tell me about last night, Diana."

With Vivian Hoy, the Torrances had rowed out to their boat, the *Brass Cupcake*, where they had been joined by a couple from a nearby boat, the Pearsons. The Pearsons had been fighting the heat for hours with gin and tonic and Phil Torrance, in order to catch up to them, began to drink with abandon. Diana had one drink. Vivian Hoy had iced tea. The athlete drank sparingly in the off season and not at all when there were games to be played. The team's victory in St. Louis was the initial topic and Phil had been lavish in his praise of Vivian Hoy. He could hardly have acted differently if he had been intent on enraging his wife. Having changed into more comfortable clothing himself on coming aboard, he suggested to Vivian that she might want to go below and get into something cooler. Since that would have meant wearing something of Diana's, Vivian refused.

"I want the boat," Phil said suddenly when he was on his third gin and tonic. "You never liked it much anyway."

Diana did not at first grasp the significance of the remark, but something in Vivian's manner alerted her. Nonetheless, she replied that she had never suggested they get rid of the boat.

It was then, lounging in a deck chair, sipping his gin and tonic, in the presence of the Pearsons and Vivian Hoy, that Phil announced that he intended to get a divorce. Diana was all but overwhelmed by the irony of the situation. She had come to the same decision, she had meant to tell Phil that night that she was leaving him, and here he was announcing to the world that he was divorcing her.

"I laughed, Sister. Where do reactions like that come from? I sounded as though I was glad. I didn't think it was at all funny that our marriage was coming to an end. Despite his running around I don't think it ever occurred to me that Phil would leave me. Yet I laughed when he said it. And when I could speak, do you know what I said? I said, 'I'll fight you for the boat. I want the boat.' You would have thought it all boiled down to which of us got possession of that stupid boat. The Pearsons were relieved at the way I acted, I think, but it was pretty clear they wanted to get back to their own boat pronto. Of course Phil wouldn't hear of it. This was a common occurrence, a suitable topic for adult conversation. Everybody gets divorced sooner or later. He reminded the Pearsons that theirs was the second marriage for each of them. He wanted to know how they had settled the boat question."

"How was Vivian Hoy taking all this?"

"She just sat there, smiling like a kitten. You may think

women athletes are muscular hunks. Vivian is lithe as a girl. And pretty. She obviously had it bad for Phil. That is when I descended to his level and suggested that all his girl friends would be delighted by the news. Oh, he was furious. Suddenly the topic lost interest for him, at least in those circumstances. He glared at me and told me he really meant what he was saying. I asked if he was referring to the boat. He got up, mad, and went into the galley for another drink. When he passed me I gave him a good shove, and over the side he went. There was a huge splash and then everyone was on his feet, staring at the water, but there was no sign of Phil. Right out loud I said, 'I hope he never comes up.' Well, a full minute went by and still he hadn't come up and it almost began to seem that he never would, as if I had control over his life. Vivian began to get excited and Pearson unbuttoned his shirt and talked of diving in and rescuing Phil. I don't know what I said to that. But that is when we heard Phil laugh.

"He must have swum under the boat. He was clambering over the side when we turned. Being dunked seemed to have restored his good spirits. His reappearance had the opposite effect on me.

"'I wish you'd drowned,' I said. They all heard me, Vivian, George and Helen Pearson. And Phil too, of course — not that it matters. Anyway, I said it and I meant it. I got into the dinghy and left.

"I don't think I slept ten consecutive minutes last night. My thoughts were murderous. And self-pitying. It infuriated me that Phil had stolen my thunder, as if *I* had given *him* cause for divorce. I paced the apartment. I raged and wept and smoked too much. I did not dare have a drink. If there ever was a time when I might have gotten drunk, last night was it. What hurt the most was that he had deliberately humiliated me in front of others. But other things, silly things, bothered me almost as much. That darned boat again. We would never have bought that boat if I hadn't wanted it. Phil thought it was just a toy and one we didn't need and I had to overcome his resistance. Later he got to like the boat so much he persuaded himself it must have been his idea we buy it. Last night I became almost hysterical with the need to make him admit how it was we had actually bought the boat.

"I was obsessed by the boat because it had become his favorite rendezvous. This morning when I went to the harbor I assumed he had spent the night on board with Vivian. I wanted to confront him again. I think I wanted to kill him. I got there just as they were fishing his body out of the water.

"I didn't realize at first it was Phil, and when I did, I felt once more that crazy urge to laugh. His falling into the water had accomplished what I said at the time I hoped it would. Given that, everyone is going to think I did it."

"Who saw you leave the boat last night?"

She seemed to think.

"They all did."

"Meaning the Pearsons, your husband, and Vivian Hoy?"

"Yes." The word emerged on exhaled smoke. "And anyone on any of the other boats who might have been interested."

"What time was it when you left?"

"I'm not sure. It was after midnight."

"And when did you arrive at your apartment?"

"I don't know. Who notices such things? And it doesn't make any difference. I have no way to prove that I went home. I could have gone back to the boat and pushed him overboard again and made sure he stayed under that time."

"Where did you leave the dinghy in which you went ashore?"

"I tied it to the clubhouse dock."

"Was it there this morning?"

"I didn't look."

"How would your husband and Vivian Hoy have gotten ashore if you had taken the dinghy?"

Diana shrugged. She seemed to be having difficulty following the conversational path Sister Mary Teresa was laying out. "That's no problem. They could have borrowed one — from the Pearsons, for example. They could swim ashore."

"How was your husband dressed when they found him?"

"He was fully dressed." She paused to puff on her cigarette. "He must have dressed again after I pushed him in."

A silence fell over the study. Sister Mary Teresa made a Christmas tree with her fat little hands on the surface of the desk and closed her eyes in thought. Both Diana and Kim waited to see what she would say. After half a minute she opened her eyes.

"You must remain here in this house until the situation clarifies. The fact that you are being sought means nothing. The wife of the deceased is being looked for. What could be more natural? It has no special significance. Where does Vivian Hoy live?"

"In town. In Chicago."

"Do you know her address?"

"It must be in the directory."

"Sister Kimberly, please look it up. Diana, go to the kitchen and ask Sister Joyce to come in here. She will make sure our guest room is ready."

"Sister, I can't stay here. I won't hide."

"A few days ago you said you wanted solitude. Now you will have a full measure of it. As soon as you leave here, you will be besieged, and it will not matter what the cause of your husband's death was."

"I have nothing to hide."

"Of course you do."

"What do you mean?" Diana looked almost shocked.

"You have all the details of your private life you have been telling me. Perhaps such things will be bruited about no matter what you do. But you do not want to have to answer questions concerning them unless it is absolutely necessary. Let us imagine that your husband accidentally drowned. A drunken man attempts to swim ashore fully clothed and doesn't make it. Perhaps that is what happened."

Something like hope flickered in Diana's eyes, then died. "Phil was an expert swimmer, drunk or sober. Besides, the Pearsons will tell the police what I did and said on the boat last night."

"None of that will matter if the drowning was accidental. Now, go fetch Sister Joyce."

Kim went with Emtee Dempsey onto the sun porch and turned on the television set.

It was just as well that Diana was not with them while they watched the news. It was clear that the death of Philip Torrance could not have been accidental. He had not died of drowning. At least it had not been a simple case of drowning. There were signs that he had been dealt a severe blow on the head before entering the water. Or so said the sources on which the facetiously knowledgeable newsman based his story. The report ended with mention that the whereabouts of Mrs. Torrance were unknown and she was being sought by the police. Emtee Dempsey turned off the set.

"Sister Kimberly, I want you to pay a call on Vivian Hoy. Find out when she left the boat and how. I want to know when she last saw Philip Torrance alive."

Kim inhaled deeply and let it out slowly, in a show of patience. "There is no reason in the world why she would answer questions put to her by me. Or by you," she added when Emtee Dempsey began to puff up. "Let the police handle it, Sister Mary Teresa."

"Diana came to me for help. I cannot ignore that."

"You are being helpful enough as it is."

"Nonsense. Do the police know that Vivian Hoy was on that boat last night?"

"They will be told by the Pearsons."

"The Pearsons could tell them, yes. I wonder if they will. You noticed that there was no mention of Chicago's star female footballer on the news."

"All the more reason why she wouldn't answer questions from me. Look, if you really want Diana to be safe and secluded here, forget about my going to see Vivian Hoy. She would tell the police, the police would come here, and then where is Diana's solitude? And you know what Richard's reaction would be."

Kim's brother Richard, a detective on the Chicago police force, was confident he would be spared purgatory in the next life because of what he suffered from Sister Mary Teresa in this one. She was forever interfering in matters that were none of her concern but that were the concern of the Chicago police department. It wasn't simply that she wished to help the police. In many instances she seemed to want to take their place. Worse, far worse, the old nun had on too many occasions seen to the bottom of cases that interested her long before the police investigation was done.

Richard's conception of humiliation and rage owed much to those sessions in the living room of the house on Walton Street when Emtee Dempsey somehow managed to show that her crazy hunches and mad hypotheses were right. Not that the old nun accepted this characterization of her procedure. She would say that nearly half a century as an historian equipped her far better than the police to get to the bottom of the deeds of men. Richard was wont to speak of the merits of scientific evidence, routine, the rules of law. Sister Mary Teresa was not opposed to such things, but she did not see why they should take precedence over common sense. And, as was true of Diana Moore Torrance,

Richard had to concede that the cases Emtee Dempsey became involved in came to her and not vice versa.

"You think Vivian Hoy would tell the police what happened on the boat last night?" the old nun asked Kim.

"Of course she would. They will already know from the Pearsons."

"And would she tell them that you went to talk with her?"

"Why wouldn't she?"

"What need to mention that a journalist had come calling on her?"

"A journalist! I will not lie to her."

Sister Mary Teresa had been leaving the porch. At Kim's remark she stopped and turned. Her brows rose above her spectacles.

"Lie? I should hope not. I want you to be absolutely candid and sincere with her. You have often expressed an admiration of Katherine Senski's distinguished career as a journalist."

"That is a far cry from wanting to be one myself."

"You are right. You are quite right. It will be better if you consider this a favor to Katherine. You will do the interview and then turn it over to Katherine. It will be an interesting departure from her usual stuff. She will be delighted to have it. With that generous intention, you can call on Vivian Hoy with a clear conscience. I am sorry that I misinterpreted your admiration for Katherine as a secret ambition."

"I'm not going."

"Of course you are. Would you want me to ask Joyce to go?"

This was moral blackmail of the worst kind. Kim could not permit Emtee Dempsey to send Joyce on this crazy errand and the old nun knew it. The trouble was that, given Joyce's interest in sports, it was tempting.

Upstairs in her room, listening to Joyce getting Diana settled down the hall, Kim tried to convince herself that all Sister

Mary Teresa really wanted was to help an old student in distress. So considered, her interest was altruistic. Putting obstacles in her way seemed suddenly small-minded and petty.

The only difficulty with this rationale was the noticeable increase in the old nun's interest after Philip Torrance's death. Richard Moriarty and his colleagues certainly could not care less if Sister Mary Teresa concerned herself with the alumnae of the College of Martha and Mary. But Kim would never be able to convince her brother that Emtee Dempsey's interest was restricted to that. In any case, by providing Diana sanctuary in the house, they were already in deeper than they should be. The thing to remember was that Diana Torrance had come of her own free will to Walton Street. Twice.

"Just ask her all about soccer," Emtee Dempsey advised when Kim checked back into the study before leaving.

"Why don't I just ask her to drop by so you can quiz her?" Kim said dryly.

"Oh, if only you could."

"What would you ask her?"

"How she killed Philip Torrance."

For a moment Emtee Dempsey looked perfectly serious, but then the twinkle returned to her eye. She held up the newspaper she had been reading. "I do not understand a word of this report on the game played in St. Louis by the Chicago Brass."

"Have Joyce explain it to you. Or better, ask Diana. After all, she's a vice president."

"I have spoken to Katherine. She is very grateful to you for undertaking this interview on her behalf. She feels that the Vivian Hoy story will fit nicely into the series of profiles she is doing on women of accomplishment."

"You actually talked with her?"

"Sister, I know you are not suggesting that I would say something that is not so. Yes, I talked with her. You may use her name. Indeed, I urge you to. I would not have you doing anything that would disturb your delicate conscience. Another thing—"

"Yes?"

"Katherine was quite *au courant* on the Philip Torrance murder."

"Murder?"

"The police are now calling it that. It seems that Diana is being sought."

"Well, well."

"You should keep in mind when you speak to Vivian Hoy that no one seems to know she was on the boat last night."

Two

Vivian Hoy lived on the twenty-first floor of a new building near the Water Tower, the interior of her studio apartment as spick and span as the building itself. A wall of window looked out at Chicago and, through a gap in the skyline, at the lake. From the lobby Kim had spoken with the athlete and, despite feeling relief because of the cover story Emtee Dempsey had contrived, felt phony palming herself off as a journalist.

"The *Tribune?*" Vivian Hoy asked, her voice over the intercom sounding remote in several senses of the word.

"The series on Women of Accomplishment. By Katherine Senski."

"And your name is Moriarity?"

"That's right."

Kim closed her eyes and crossed her fingers. Now that it was proving somewhat difficult to see Vivian Hoy she found herself wanting very much to talk to the footballer. This was the woman who had witnessed the events on the boat of which Diana had told them.

"Well, come on up." She spoke with obvious reluctance.

Going up in the elevator, which rose with a vertiginous swiftness, Kim thought it odd that Vivian Hoy should be less than eager to see the press. She had not thought athletes were shy about interviews.

Vivian Hoy was a silhouette when she opened the door to Kim. The windows with their wonderful view were bright with sun, and Kim came blinking into the apartment feeling uncomfortably like a burglar caught in the glare of a flashlight. She realized that Vivian Hoy had extended her hand. They shook and, with her eyes growing accustomed to the glare, Kim followed the woman past the dining alcove to the sitting area. Commenting on the view, Kim felt she was following a script for those first visiting the room.

"Isn't it great? I've been in the apartment nearly two years and I'm still not used to it. I can stand there by the hour just staring. I'm a native of Davenport."

Perhaps there was something of the corn-fed Iowa maid about her that the remark suggested, but Kim was struck by the self-assurance and authority in the pale blue eyes. Vivian wore white slacks and a solid green blouse. Her reddish hair was cut short and worn in a bang over her eyes.

"Smoke if you want to," Vivian said when Kim was comfortable in a chair.

"No thanks."

Kim assumed that Vivian Hoy was merely being polite and was surprised when the athlete lit a cigarette.

"I'd appreciate it if you didn't mention the smoking. I promised the Torrances I'd keep it quiet."

"The Torrances?" The question seemed worse than a lie.

"They own the Brass."

"The man who was found dead this morning?"

Vivian Hoy would have flunked out of acting school if her effort to look surprised was the best she could summon. Since Kim could not question the sincerity of that surprise, she was cast in the role of the one to tell Vivian Hoy that her employer's body had been found floating in Belmont Harbor that morning.

"My God!"

"When did you last see him?"

"I saw him last night. We flew back from St. Louis. The team. Phil travels with us."

"I hate to be the one to tell you this."

"Do the rest of the players know?"

"I haven't any idea."

"Somebody should be thinking of what this will do to the team. I suppose Eileen is. She's our executive secretary. Eileen West."

"What will it do?"

"I don't know. It's a big question mark. Who will run things now? Diana?" She looked quickly at Kim and failed another acting lesson. "I must sound awful, wondering about the team when a man is dead. Tell me the details. What happened to Phil? How did he drown?"

Kim might have played along with the pretense but she had to face Emtee Dempsey when she went back to Walton Street and the old nun would have been unforgiving if Kim had permitted Vivian Hoy to carry on as if all this was news to her. So she hit the young woman with whatever a foul in soccer is called.

"We've been picking up rumors that you were with Philip Torrance last night."

"I was. I told you. He and his wife drove me home from the airport."

"Directly?"

"What do you mean?"

"Did you stop by his boat in Belmont Harbor? Our sources speak of a party on Torrance's boat late last night."

"Who are your sources?"

"Journalists never give away their sources, Vivian. You know that."

"It's her, isn't it? Diana?" Vivian shook her head and looked sad, genuinely sad. "Did she say she was at the party too?"

"Then there was a party on the boat?"

"Don't ask me. If there was one, I wasn't at it. And you'll have trouble finding anyone besides her who would say I was there."

"Do you know a couple named Pearson?"

"Who are they?"

"They have a boat too. It was anchored near the Torrance boat."

"Were they at the party you mentioned?"

"All we have is rumors, of course."

"If they were there, they can tell you I wasn't."

"The Torrances drove you directly from the airport to this building last night?"

Vivian looked as if she were beginning to wonder at the direction of Kim's questions.

"Believe me, I don't like being the one to tell you about Mr. Torrance," Kim said.

"I still can't believe he's dead."

"You knew him pretty well?"

"I worked for him. As I said, he traveled with the team. Sure I knew him."

"What was he like?"

Her smile was crooked but attractive. "A water boy. You must know the type. They can't play anything worth a darn themselves, but they can't keep away from the game. Any game.

And they know more about a sport than the people who play it. Gung ho. That's the word for Phil Torrance. His whole life was the Chicago Brass."

"He and his wife owned it?"

Vivian Hoy nodded, her eyes pulled toward the skyline.

"What is she like?"

"Your source? I should ask you that question."

"You don't like her the way you did her husband?"

"Look." Vivian Hoy moved to the edge of her seat. "She was jealous. Imagine. I've told you what Phil was like. Okay. Not exactly the answer to a maiden's prayer. Besides, he's middle-aged. He's like my father, if anything. And his wife thinks something is going on? She's crazy."

"She thought something was going on between you and Philip Torrance?"

"It sounds silly when you say it aloud, doesn't it? But she claimed to believe it. Not that Phil was perfect."

"What do you mean?"

"I think he did cheat on Diana. Oh, I'm sure he did. It was pretty common knowledge on the team. So why did she have to pick on me? She had a lot of real rivals if she wanted to pick a fight."

Vivian, who had been looking out the window as much as at Kim, now concentrated on her visitor. "Why am I telling you all this, for heaven's sake? Now, what is this series you talked about?"

Kim had scarcely begun describing the series on women of achievement that Katherine Senski was writing for the *Tribune* when there was the sound of the bell ringing. Vivian frowned and shrugged and picked up the telephone. It was the police calling from the lobby. Vivian looked at Kim as if for advice, and for a moment she did look like a girl from Davenport, Iowa, lost in the big city. Kim, who had not yet taken from her purse the notepad that was to serve as her prop for the interview, started to rise.

"Would you mind staying. I think we both know what this is about."

Kim suddenly wondered if Vivian had friends she could call to be with her now. Whatever the truth of Diana's story about Vivian, the athlete was in for some grueling days ahead as the death of Philip Torrance was investigated by the police and the newspapers. She agreed to stay. It seemed the least she could do for someone she was being less than completely honest with.

When Vivian opened the door, Kim could see the man standing there react to the light from the window as she herself had. Her sigh of relief must have been audible to Vivian. For a mad moment Kim had been perfectly prepared to find it was her brother Richard, come to question Vivian Hoy, only to find his sister already on the scene.

"This is Kim Moriarity," Vivian Hoy explained.

"Officer Gleason," he said, flashing a badge. Behind him stood another cop. The studio apartment was going to be crowded with the four of them in it.

"Moriarity?" Gleason, thirtyish, well over six feet, wore his thin hair brushed forward over a furrowed brow.

"A journalist," Vivian said.

"What paper?" the other, O'Connell, asked. Short and fat, he looked like the runt of a litter, with narrow eyes, a pointed nose, and an unconvincing smile.

"The *Tribune*," Vivian answered for her. "Anyone care for a drink? Maybe a beer?"

The two detectives refused with the primness of altar boys. Kim was relieved to have their attention diverted.

O'Connell said, "You the Hoy that plays for the Brass?"

"That's right."

"You heard the news?" Gleason asked.

"Just before you got here. Kim..."

Again two pairs of eyes were turned on Kim. Gleason seemed to be thinking he knew her. If he made the connection with the house on Walton Street, school was out. Not that it made any difference. Richard would surely hear that Kim Moriarity had been in Vivian Hoy's apartment when the police arrived.

Kim said, "What took you so long to get here?"

"What's that supposed to mean?" O'Connell wanted to know.

"Philip Torrance's body was found this morning. It is now ..." She looked at her watch. "It is now going on three P.M."

"Sister Mary Teresa!" O'Connell burst out. He nodded as if in agreement with himself, then cast a disgusted look at Gleason. "She's Moriarity's sister."

"Jesus, Mary, and Joseph."

"What are you doing here?" O'Connell growled.

Gleason said, "What's this malarkey about the *Tribune*?"

The expression on Vivian Hoy's face made Kim feel like a traitor.

"Aren't you a journalist?" Vivian asked.

"I agreed to interview you and to give the rights to the interview to Katherine Senski...."

"She's a nun," Gleason said.

"A nun!"

Vivian Hoy's eyes, huge in repose, grew wider still.

O'Connell said, "Granted she doesn't look like one. Not many do anymore. Sister Mary Teresa now, there's a real nun."

Vivian Hoy collapsed into a chair and just stared at the three of them, but her look was one of reproach when she turned to Kim.

"You're really a nun?"

Kim nodded. "I know this sounds just awful. I haven't been completely open with you but there really is a Katherine Senski and she really does want to include you in her series. Still, the visit was a ruse."

"You came to talk to me about Phil Torrance?"

"Yes."

"Why?"

This was oddly the most difficult part. "Diana Torrance is an alumna of our college."

She could see the curtain ring down in Vivian's mind. Kim was now firmly located with the enemy. Vivian turned to the police as to comparative friends. Kim did not regret having told Vivian about Diana. She felt terrible about being discovered in such a hoax and for a moment she bitterly resented Sister Mary Teresa's sedentary curiosity. All *she* had to do was sit in her study in the house on Walton Street and shag Kim around town to assuage her curiosity about whatever. It was demeaning. Well, perhaps. But Kim was a grown woman who could have said No. It wasn't a matter of religious obedience. It was a favor. So she had owed the explanation to Vivian and she wouldn't blame the woman if she never spoke to her again. "I'll be going," Kim said.

"Stick around," Gleason barked.

"I will not," Kim said. "I can leave if I want to."

"What are you really doing here?" O'Connell asked. "Your brother is going to want to know."

"He knows where to find me." To Vivian Hoy, Kim said, "I'm sorry."

Vivian Hoy made a little face. "I went to school to the nuns." It was unclear what that was supposed to mean.

"You don't have to talk to these two if you don't want to."

"Why wouldn't I talk to them?"

Gleason said, "I thought you were going."

"Sister," O'Connell added.

Kim went. She closed the door of the apartment, shutting

off the light; she dropped swiftly down to the ground level on the too-fast elevator, and went like a zombie through the lobby. She had never felt quite so foolish in her life, and again she wanted to blame it on Emtee Dempsey. At a pay phone in the lobby, she stopped. Hers was a message best given by phone. Joyce answered and immediately put her through to Emtee Dempsey.

"What did you learn?"

"To trust my own instincts."

"Things went badly?"

"It was a disaster."

"In what way?"

Kim told her in what way, in detail. Like most horrors, this one was exorcised somewhat in the telling. She found she could not convey to Emtee Dempsey the embarrassment she had felt when the police identified her and she had to explain herself to Vivian Hoy.

"There is no basis for embarrassment. You said nothing untrue. And you were even more frank when the occasion called for it."

"But I became the enemy."

"Hmmm. And what about last night?" It helped to get away from her humiliation and back to the time she had had alone with Vivian before the police arrived. Emtee Dempsey was particularly interested in Kim's feeling that Vivian was simulating ignorance of Philip Torrance's death.

"She denied being on the boat?"

"Her story was that she did not know Phil Torrance was dead, she had not been with him and Diana and the Pearsons on the boat, and the last time she saw him was when the Torrances dropped her off at her apartment after Diana picked her and Philip Torrance up at O'Hare when they returned with the Chicago Brass from St. Louis. She never heard of the Pearsons."

"You must go talk to them now."

A black man in a species of uniform — navy blue suit with brass buttons — stood behind a counter in the lobby, able to hear every word she said and trying to look as if he couldn't. Kim made a face at Emtee Dempsey's last remark and the man smiled at her. She smiled back, and for the rest of the call she was shrugging and smiling and lifting her eyes to heaven for the benefit of the security man while trying to convince Sister Mary Teresa that she was not going down to Belmont Harbor and talk with the Pearsons.

"Is there a directory where you are calling from, Sister?" There was, wonderful to say; another sign of the newness of the building and the conscientiousness of the security people. Emtee Dempsey told her to look up Pearson in the book. "Are you there?"

"There are almost two pages of Pearsons in the book."

"I will ask Diana for his first name. I've forgotten it."

"Sister, I am not..."

She stopped when she heard the phone being put down on the desk top. If Emtee Dempsey would now go down the hallway to the kitchen and ask Joyce to get Diana, or, worse, herself climb the stairs to the guest room, Kim could be standing in the lobby of Vivian Hoy's building for more than five minutes holding a dead phone. From across the lobby the black security man smiled at her. Kim began to talk into the dead phone. She had felt ridiculous and ashamed upstairs when Vivian Hoy had learned who she really was, but now she felt worse than silly. How in the world did actors manage to carry on with a telephone prop as if there were someone at the other end of the line? Kim felt she was being far less convincing than Vivian Hoy when the soccer player had professed not to know of Philip Torrance's death. The security man looked away, as if he was as embarrassed as she was.

"That isn't the way it is at all," Kim said into the phone, contributing to an imaginary conversation. She tipped back her head and closed her eyes, as if concentrating on what she was listening to. "I do not believe this," she said aloud. To say that a phone is dead does not mean that it delivers no sounds. Kim became aware of remote impassioned conversations and had the sense that she was eavesdropping on neighboring wires. How busy the air was with the troubles and business of men. "This is the most ridiculous thing I have ever done," she said into the receiver.

"What are you doing?" Joyce asked. Kim gave a little jump at the sound of her voice.

"Where did she go?"

"Emtee Dempsey?"

"Yes. I am standing in the lobby of a building holding a public phone..."

"It's George and Helen Pearson."

"Do you know what she expects me to do?"

"Sure. Visit the Pearsons at Belmont Harbor. Did you talk with Vivian Hoy?"

"Yes."

"What's she like?"

"I'll tell you tonight."

"Tonight we're going to see the Brass play the Boston Flutter." Her life seemed to be planned in detail by someone else. Did anyone care that she had planned to return to the Northwestern library? Emtee Dempsey, the great champion of scholarship, insisted that Kim must earn her doctorate in history, they would decide later what she would then do, but when the chips were down, any whim of the old nun's took precedence over her studies. She told Joyce she had to hang up or they would make her sign a lease. The security man skipped out from behind his little counter and held the door open for her. His smile looked genuine now. No doubt he was glad to see her go. Outside, the wind came whipping in from the direction of the lake and despite the sun Kim was glad she had her coat on. She buttoned it, lowered her head, and started into the wind. Michigan Avenue was two blocks away, and by the time she reached it Kim decided to have a cup of coffee before catching a cab for Belmont Harbor. She bought the latest edition of the paper before going into the coffee house, where she sat at the counter and caught up on the public version of the mess she was allowing herself to get involved with.

To the untutored eye, the story seemed straightforward, laced with just enough journalistic rhetoric to keep the jaded reader's eye. Philip Torrance might have been surprised to find himself described as a wealthy socialite and his ownership of the Chicago Brass as a minor avocation. Perhaps it was because he had died after spending the evening on his anchored boat that suggested the line. In any case, Torrance came through as a sort of playboy whose death by drowning could not be accepted as the accident it had first been thought to be. Why not? Among other things, Torrance was known to be an excellent swimmer. For another, he was unlikely to have been in the water last night intentionally. The idea that he had decided to go ashore by swimming was discarded as fanciful. The autopsy showed that Torrance had been drinking heavily. But the decisive thing was the evidence of a blow to the head. Mrs. Torrance was said to be in seclusion. Had Emtee Dempsey conveyed something to Katherine Senski about Diana Moore Torrance's whereabouts? The mention of Mrs. Torrance spared the police one embarrassment, even if they did not know where the new widow was.

There was only the most fleeting mention of the women's soccer team. "Mr. Torrance had a financial interest in the women's professional soccer team, the Chicago Brass." The sentence did not begin to convey the passionate obsession Diana had spoken of. It occurred to Kim that not much of what Diana had told Emtee Dempsey seemed corroborated from other sources.

Had her own reaction to Vivian Hoy's apparent ignorance of what had happened to Philip Torrance been the result of having heard Diana first?

Belmont Harbor, on the near north side, is a natural basin improved by art, in which several hundred boats bob on the waters of Lake Michigan, within minutes of their owners' offices and homes. Few urban sailors have as much ease in pursuing their passion as does the Chicago sailor. From the offices of the Chicago Brass in the Hancock Building it would have taken Philip Torrance perhaps fifteen minutes to be aboard his boat. From his apartment on Dempster it was half that. The world of sailing was as foreign to Kim as it could possibly be. All her life she had been aware of boats on the lake: freighters, barges, powerboats, and, far more beautiful, the sailing craft, their great triangular sheets filling with wind and carrying them eastward into the vastness of Lake Michigan. These boats had simply been there, as much parts of the landscape as birds and trees. She had not thought of them as things to be constantly fussed over, to be rigged and readied and sailed with love and, the sailing done, fussed over even more.

She skirted the boathouse and went to the dock where several people were visible. Too late she recognized her brother Richard. If their eyes had not met, she would have turned and left, hoping he would think he had to be mistaken; his sister the nun could not possibly be intruding on the scene of a suspicious death, not after the fraternal scolding he had given her on the last occasion of Emtee Dempsey's trespassing on his work.

"Kim! Kim, wait!"

She had turned and started back the way she had come but there was little point in thinking she could escape. He ran up to her, coat open, tie flapping in the breeze, the red hair twisted from the wind. His smile had menace in it.

"What the hell are you doing here?"

"What am I *doing* here?" Kim looked around. "Is this some private preserve? I thought it was a public place."

"Kim, cut it out. Gleason and O'Connell have already reported you were visiting Vivian Hoy. I want to know why."

"And I don't owe you an answer, as you very well know."

If he had an Irish temper, so did she, and they had gotten them from the same source. Richard looked over his shoulder to see if her sassy reply had been heard by his colleagues. Apparently not. That calmed him somewhat.

"Kim, a simple answer to a simple question. What is Emtee Dempsey's interest in the death of Philip Torrance?"

Kim thought a bit and then decided it was safe to tell him that Philip Torrance was married to a woman who had graduated from their college

"I didn't think she had become a soccer fan."

"What happened to Torrance, Richard?"

"He died."

"Was he murdered?" He squinted at her, tall, freckled, good-looking, or so she thought.

"Why do you ask that?"

"Because you're here, obviously. Because Gleason and O'Connell showed up at Vivian Hoy's when I was talking with her."

"About what?"

"Her career. I'm helping Katherine Senski on a profile of Vivian."

The thing about Emtee Dempsey's ploys was that the more you said them, the less implausible they sounded.

"That was your only reason for being there?" His voice was heavy with incredulity.

"Richard, she didn't even know that Torrance was dead."

"You're kidding."

"And I had to be the one to tell her."

"When did you find out? Don't tell me. Katherine Senski called and had the perfect excuse for you to pay a call on Vivian Hoy. So what brings you here? Did you plan to row out to the Torrance boat and look around?"

"Which one is it?" He turned and pointed, accompanying the gesture with instructions on where she was to look. And then she had it. She didn't know what she had expected, but somehow she was disappointed. It rode low in the water and its high mast seemed disproportionate to its length. The movement of the mast was mesmeric, to and fro, to and fro, an inverted pendulum keeping a time that would no longer measure the activities of Philip Torrance.

"Which boat is the Pearsons'?"

"Who the hell are the Pearsons?"

"George and Helen. I'm told their boat is docked close to the Torrances'."

"Told by whom?"

"Have you spoken with them?"

"I never heard of them. And we have been questioning anyone and everyone around here who could give us any information. Just a minute." Richard strode back to the men he had left to come after her. She saw the heads cock as he spoke and then the pause before they shook them back and forth. By then Kim would have bet on it. She met Richard halfway.

"No Pearsons?" she said helpfully.

"Who told you about them?"

"Their name came up when I was talking with Vivian Hoy." And then it hit him, the big eureka. There was everything but a light bulb appearing over Richard's head.

"She's with you, isn't she? On Walton Street? Mrs. Torrance. Honest to God!"

This time he left her on the run, in the direction of the street. Kim headed for the boathouse, hopeful of finding a pay phone there. The most she could do was give Emtee Dempsey and Joyce a warning they were about to have company.

"We'll get her out of the house," Joyce said.

"Let Emtee Dempsey decide."

"You're kidding."

Kim hung up, left the boathouse, and strode up to the street. It was nearly fifteen minutes later when she arrived at the house on Walton Street. Richard's car was parked at the curb.

When she closed the front door behind her, she could hear him talking. He was in the living room, standing before Emtee Dempsey, who sat enthroned in a brocade chair, looking up at him through her rimless glasses as if he were a member of some species with which she had no previous acquaintance.

"I will by God get a warrant and search these premises, Sister Mary Teresa. I am absolutely serious about that."

"Richard Moriarity, you are welcome to look through this house without a warrant. Here is Sister Kimberly to show you about. I must say, however, that a more sensitive person than I would resent the implications of this search."

"In what way?"

"Why, one would think you did not believe me when I say that the person you seek is not here. Mrs. Torrance, wasn't it?" Perhaps if she had not pretended to be unsure of the object of Richard's quest he would have forgotten about searching the house.

"Mrs. Philip Torrance," Richard said fiercely. "Her husband's body was found this morning."

Richard seemed to get angrier when his eyes met Kim's.

She said, "You might have given me a ride."

"Show your brother around, Sister Kimberly," Emtee Dempsey said, levering herself to her feet with her cane. "I must get back to work." And off she went to her study while Kim showed Richard around. They started in the basement, where there was a small apartment that had once housed the help. He checked the closets and under the bed, avoiding her eyes. Upstairs, in the chapel, Kim paused to say a prayer, but Richard, satisfied that only God was in the chapel, was anxious to continue the search. He went on to the kitchen, where Joyce offered him a cup of coffee.

"Do you have a beer?"

"I thought you were on duty."

"All the more reason." It was pretty clear that he realized he would not be getting this Cook's tour if they had anything to hide, but he meant to go through with it anyway. Perhaps taking the beer was meant to add a festive note, as if they all understood this was merely for the record. When they came downstairs after a quick check of the second floor — Kim was relieved to see that the guest room bore no signs of Diana's occupancy — Richard turned to her.

"Was she here, Kim?"

"Diana Torrance?"

"Diana Torrance," he repeated with exaggerated patience.

"Yes. Yes, she was here a few days ago to visit Sister Mary Teresa. I think I told you Mrs. Torrance is an alumna of our college. She took classes from Sister Mary Teresa. It was that visit that made all of us so concerned when we heard of the death of Mr. Torrance."

"I'll bet. And that's why you dropped in on Vivian Hoy. Or is she an alumna of the college too?"

"She's far too young to have attended the college, Richard."

"Yeah."

"Come on in the kitchen and finish your beer." Joyce left them alone, which was unnecessary. If Richard didn't want to talk to her about the death of Philip Torrance he wouldn't do it, whether Joyce was present or not. But he was willing to talk. Perhaps it was the wild-goose chase of this visit to Walton Street and the need to redeem himself in his own eyes if not in hers that made him sit at the kitchen table and tell Kim what they knew and did not know of the death of Philip Torrance.

The Chicago Brass had played in St. Louis the day before and had returned to Chicago, arriving at eleven-ten. Mrs. Torrance had picked up her husband at O'Hare and the speculation was that they had gone home and then he had decided to go to the boat; maybe they had had a quarrel, maybe he just wanted to be on the boat. By all reports he had been an avid sailor and was especially proud of his boat. He was also a pretty good drinker and a boat at anchor is a bar afloat. Philip Torrance had had an inordinate number of drinks. His body had been found with a serious lesion in the head, near the main wharf, just below the boathouse, at six that morning by a young man, Jason Smally, who had come down to take out his Laser.

"That's a small one-man boat," Richard explained, repeating what he had been told; he was as much of a landlubber as Kim. "Very popular."

"It all sounds like an accident, Richard. The man got drunk and fell into the water and drowned."

"Yes, if there hadn't been a gash at the back of his head."

"Couldn't he have struck it on something?"

"The coroner does not think death was due to drowning. Certainly not to drowning alone. Whoever conked Torrance on the head is responsible for his death."

"But who would want him dead?"

Richard pursed his lips and poured the rest of the beer into his glass. "A surprising number of people. The more we question, the more possibilities turn up."

Philip Torrance had not achieved success without making enemies. His methods could be described as ruthless. He had made enemies in his previous jobs, but they had become legion since he had founded the Chicago Brass.

"He and his wife gave the impression that they were the exclusive owners — he the president, she the vice president. That isn't true. There are three other partners, one silent by choice, two others who feel that Torrance turned the team into a private toy and made all kinds of decisions without consulting them as he should have. The fact that the guy had the Midas touch did not make it easier to take. Maybe it made it harder."

"Who *are* the partners, Richard?"

"A couple named Evans. His name is Eugene. They are the unwillingly silent partners. The real silent partner is Norman Shire."

"Who is he?"

"A sports writer. You can see why he wouldn't want it known that he owns part of a team. Well, everyone is going to know it now. The funny thing is that Shire used his column to lambast Philip Torrance. The fact that he may have been writing as a disgruntled partner takes on interest, given the circumstances of Torrance's death."

"That's three suspects." Kim held up three fingers.

"There are more, as I said. Torrance was not exactly a faithful husband. In fact, he had a deserved reputation as a chaser. The fact that a woman was married never deterred him, apparently. There is a platoon of irate husbands for whom the thought of Torrance dead may not lead to uncontrolled grief."

"Plus a large number of cast-off female partners."

"Yes. And of course all this must have been very painful to his wife."

"You think she knew about his infidelity?"

"Everybody knew about it."

"If his death is due to the blow that was struck him, it must have happened at the harbor."

"It happened on the boat. We found traces of blood. We have divers looking for the weapon."

"A blunt instrument?"

He glared at her. "One guess is a winch."

"I see."

"It's a kind of wrench. So it's murder, and that's why I get angry when I find you snooping around, getting involved in matters that among other things are dangerous." Richard pushed back his chair and stood.

"Try to get you-know-who to understand that, Kim. I don't want to have you showing up anywhere else in this investigation just because Mrs. Torrance is a former student of Emtee Dempsey. Half the town are former students of hers."

"That's a bit of an exaggeration."

She went to the front door with him and watched him stride out to his car. There was something of their father in the set of his shoulders and in the way he walked, just as their mother's sardonic humor got into his eyes when he was not angry. Kim was proud of her big brother. Once, before the Order had seemingly collapsed, he had been proud of her. Maybe he still was. She could hardly blame him for resenting the way in which Sister Mary Teresa kept intruding in his official work. Kim went down the hallway to the study and tapped on the door.

"Come in." The old nun's voice did not sound annoyed at being disturbed. No wonder. Kim entered the study to find Diana Moore Torrance seated across the desk from Sister Mary Teresa.

Three

Kim stood there with her mouth hanging open and felt a tremor of terror at what Richard's reaction would have been if he had decided to check out the study too before he left. The expression on Sister Mary Teresa's face was a bit devilish, but Diana, to her credit, looked both sheepish and apologetic.

"Has Richard gone?" Emtee Dempsey asked.

Kim ignored her and spoke to Diana. "Have you been here all along?"

"I slipped out the back door and went to the corner for cigarettes. Are the police still looking for me?"

"Yes."

Kim squared her shoulders and took a deep breath. Calmness is all. "Diana, forget about the police. Your husband is dead. Arrangements are going to have to be made."

"We have, of course, discussed all that," Sister Mary Teresa said. "Diana has authorized Mr. Rush to take care of matters for her. Please don't add to her burden by suggesting that she is being remiss in her obligations as a widow."

"Widow." Diana repeated the word wonderingly. She must at times have imagined its application to herself, but this was real. Her husband was dead. After twenty years she was alone again. Her eyes grew moist with self-pitying tears.

"Who are the Pearsons?" Kim demanded. Her excursion had made her doubtful of Diana and the sudden tears seemed as much tactic as emotion. "The couple who joined you and your husband and Vivian Hoy on the boat last night," she added, when Diana looked confused.

"Just a couple from a nearby boat. Did you ask Vivian about them?"

"She denies having been on the boat, so obviously she can't be expected to identify the couple."

Diana shook her head. "What earthly difference does it make? I'm sorry I even mentioned them."

"You must have realized that they could vouch for your having left the boat when you said you did."

"You act as if I had invented them."

"As I remember, you said your husband referred to the fact that the Pearsons had both been married before. He must have known them. Did you?"

"They weren't friends, no."

"Had you seen them before?"

"Oh, I'm sure I had. There are always so many people who come and go when you have a boat. As you say, Phil seemed to know things about them I didn't."

"Vivian Hoy's version of last night does not comport with Diana's, I gather," Sister Mary Teresa said.

Kim gave her a detailed report of the visit, stressing the differences between the athlete's account and what they had heard from Diana. The latter's vagueness about the Pearsons had strengthened Kim's suspicion that this was one old student of Emtee Dempsey's who could teach her teacher a thing or two about deception. And the importance of the Pearsons became yet more obvious in the telling. Without them, Diana's story about going to the boat would be without corroboration.

"Wouldn't someone at the harbor have noticed the arrival of the three of you at that hour? And have heard the party going on while the Pearsons were there? Did you see anyone when you left the boat?"

It was sufficient to ask these questions to see from Diana's expression that she had no useful answers to them.

Sister Mary Teresa cleared her throat importantly, hitched forward on her chair, and took over. They needed outside advice and that, as so often in the past, meant Katherine Senski. Emtee Dempsey pushed the phone toward Kim and asked her to get in touch with Katherine.

"Sister, it is nearly five in the afternoon."

"Have her come for a drink. Katherine likes a drink at the end of the day."

"Is that all you want me to say?"

Emtee Dempsey thought for a moment. "Tell her to come join the brass for some grog."

This cryptic message, which Kim refused to interpret, proved irresistible to Katherine. A minute or two past five-thirty she got out of a cab and came flouncing toward the door of the house on Walton Street.

Kim had been on the lookout for her as Joyce had gone off to buy ingredients for the drinks Emtee Dempsey had been promising both Katherine and Diana. Diana brightened at the prospect of a drink. It was a martini that she craved, but when she had to explain that this drink was made of gin she said, "I'll mix it myself."

"As you wish," said Emtee Dempsey sweetly, apparently

not catching the implication of the offer. Joyce did, Kim was sure, and she could not have appreciated any aspersions cast on her competence in the kitchen or environs. Katherine would drink either beer or sauterne, depending, though what the choice depended on Kim could not have said. The woman who mounted the steps shortly after five-thirty did not look like someone who would be indecisive for long.

Katherine had less clothes sense than a Trappistine, certainly a lot less than most nuns now dressing in ordinary garb. Kim in her khaki skirt and polka-dot blouse felt like a fashion plate by comparison. Katherine's dress was the kind worn by all one's grandaunts in the old photographs found in attics. Today Katherine wore what she described as her blue faille, a shapeless tent of cloth relieved at the throat by a little white collar and a huge rope of marble-sized beads. Katherine was half again as tall as Emtee Dempsey but she was proportionately overweight. She did not like the old nun using a cane, but the way she mounted the steps suggested that she would be wise to get one of her own. Her face brightened when Kim opened the door just as she came up on the porch.

"Aha. I seem to be awaited." She gave Kim a quick kiss on the cheek. "What's it all about?"

"Ask Sister Mary Teresa."

"It's about Philip Torrance," Katherine said, heading toward the study. "It's got to be."

So the use of the term brass had conveyed what it was meant to.

Sister Mary Teresa was on her feet when Katherine entered, and after presenting Diana to the somewhat startled journalist, she suggested they adjourn to the living room. The study could accommodate three comfortably but beyond that it got a little cramped.

"I was sorry to hear about your husband," Katherine said.

Diana looked tragic. "I am still too numb to believe it."

"Terrible thing," Katherine muttered, but Kim saw that those wise old eyes were studying Diana with interest.

Settled into a chair, Katherine lit a cigarette, as did Diana. Only the slightest twitch of her nostrils indicated how offensive Emtee Dempsey found cigarette smoke. It was not a topic on which she was given to elaborate, however. The idea that the use of tobacco is what is wrong with the modern world struck the old nun as one of those idiocies that gave credence to the notion that Western civilization is in steep and irreversible decline. She had once suggested a federal warning to be printed on all packages whatsoever: Entropy is dangerous to your health.

"Are you in hiding here?" Katherine asked abruptly.

Diana looked at Emtee Dempsey. "I'm a guest."

"I suggested she stay, Katherine. In a moment you will understand why."

"I was a student of Sister's," Diana said.

"That is not the reason," Emtee Dempsey said with smiling toleration. "Tell Katherine about last night."

The story Diana told was the story she had told them earlier in the day. Doubtless it was just because she was hearing it a second time that Kim thought it sounded rehearsed, the whole thing a prepared tale. But she had to concede that Diana told of the events in such a way that Kim felt herself to be an eyewitness of them. As she had that morning, as Katherine clearly did now, Kim had the vivid sense of being on the boat in Belmont harbor when Philip Torrance so cruelly told his wife he intended to leave her.

"Why did you return to the harbor this morning?" Katherine asked.

"I just had to. I felt it was all unfinished business."

They were interrupted by the entrance of Joyce with the tray of drinks. She had gone ahead and prepared them when she returned from the liquor store to forestall the invasion of her terrain by Diana. Diana sipped her drink tentatively, sipped it again, and nodded approval. "Very good, Sister. Very good."

Katherine drained half her glass of wine, leaned forward to set it on the table in front of her chair, and looked over her glasses at Diana.

"You were wrong to accept the invitation to stay here, Mrs. Torrance. Your story has a prima facie implausibility, and for you to be mysteriously unfindable at the same time puts you in a most precarious position. Naming no names, I am surprised that a certain mutual friend entertained for a moment the thought of your dropping out of sight."

"The idea was mine," Diana said. "Originally."

"That is some consolation at least. You should go immediately to the telephone and call the police."

"You can of course tell them that you have been staying here," Emtee Dempsey said placidly as if she were not being criticized. She fished a watch from a pocket under the white starched bib-like garment that covered her chest, pressed its stem, and frowned. "It has been somewhere between nine and twelve hours since the body of your husband was found floating in the lake."

A little gasp from Diana and uneasy stirring from Katherine greeted this.

"Surely no one could be surprised that, having come here for a day of meditation and retreat, you should just now be able to respond to the dreadful news of your husband's death. I think I should make that call for you. Sister Kimberly?"

Kim could never understand how Emtee managed to maneuver others into situations where she herself was the dramatic center of things. After Kim had brought the phone to the old nun, feeding out line from its normal station in the corner, and dialed the number, they all seemed to sit forward in their chairs in hushed anticipation of what would happen next. Who but Sister Mary Teresa could make a simple phone call seem the dramatic equivalent of a declaration of World War III?

"Hello? Hello? I would like to speak with Lieutenant Richard Moriarity, please."

Richard, dear God! Suddenly this seemed worse than World War III to Kim. They had gone through an elaborate ruse to prove to Richard that Diana was not here. How on earth could Emtee Dempsey now expect him to accept the tale implicit in her remarks before she had phoned?

"Richard? This is Sister Mary Teresa. Yes. There is something I wanted to tell you personally, as I know it will come as a great relief to you. You were looking for Mrs. Philip Torrance? She is here. Yes, right here on Walton Street. We are at this very moment seated in the living room. The first thing mentioned was that you should be informed and that is what I am doing. Could you join us?"

She had been speaking with her eyes closed, as if only darkness could provide the appropriate setting for responding to the vertiginous gyroscope she used to keep on the sunny side of the line dividing truth from falsity. After her suggestion that Richard might like to stop by Walton Street, her eyes popped open. She removed the receiver from her starched headdress and looked at it in a somewhat startled way. Then she returned it to its cradle. She looked at the others.

"I believe he meant he will be with us directly."

"You have the nerve of a burglar," Katherine said, not without admiration in her voice.

"Katherine, it was your suggestion that the police be informed. You shall receive full credit for it. It was, needless to say, an excellent idea, which is why I acted on it as soon as you expressed it."

"You neglected to mention that Diana was here when we persuaded him she wasn't," Kim said in a level voice. No matter how outrageous Emtee Dempsey was, she was the one who would catch it from Richard.

"Can I tell them I have been here all day?"

"Can you?" Sister Mary Teresa looked shocked. "You must. There must be absolutely no tampering with the truth. You must be candid and forthcoming with the police. They have the personnel and equipment and experience to solve this mystery, and every bit of information you provide them will enhance their efforts."

"I'm not hearing this," Joyce said in disbelief, as well she might. Emtee Dempsey's normal attitude toward a police investigation was not so much one of contempt as Olympian amusement at the thought that routine and allegedly scientific procedures could substitute for the time-honored use of practical reason whereby men had always confronted the problematic. Richard could speak dismissively of hunches and intuitions. Emtee Dempsey was not the champion of the irrational but of the sense of rational that antedated the many and wondrous instruments of modern criminal investigation. Psychology? Not in any current understanding of the term. If pressed, Emtee Dempsey would go on and on, with many learned references to Aristotle, Pascal, and Cardinal Newman. Joyce's remark brought the old nun's eyes swinging around to her.

"Sister Joyce is an avid fan of the Chicago Brass," she said musingly, as if seeking some inspiration in the remark.

"Oh, no you don't," Joyce said.

"Don't what?" Emtee Dempsey still wore a half-expectant expression.

"I didn't ask Mrs. Torrance to stay. I know what you're thinking. We started to talk about the team and one thing led to another and before you know it it's going on six, Katherine is here, and suggests we call the police because Mrs. Torrance just remembered her husband died this morning."

Joyce almost certainly had not meant her remark as a criticism of Diana, but she had, however heedlessly, said a significant thing. Diana Moore Torrance's reaction to her husband's death was certainly unusual. That it might have occurred to her to come immediately to Walton Street from Belmont Harbor that morning when she learned her husband had drowned was one thing. She had been here a few days before, the house was not all that far from the harbor. But that she should have stayed here all day, whether on her own initiative or someone else's, was startling. Yet Kim had not really been surprised until Katherine, coming in from the real world, had pointed it out.

Diana, as if recognizing that she must say something, looked into the drink she held with both hands. "Sister Mary Teresa knows why I came here to ask her advice a few days ago. You all know the humiliation I suffered last night. None of you knows what it is like to be married, I think. Perhaps the best of marriages are difficult truces. I know what my own was like. I would like to say that I feel grief, that Philip's death wipes away the memory of all the things he did to me, but it hasn't. It is a dreadful thing to say, especially here, to you, but my first reaction to the realization that Philip was dead was relief. Almost glee. There is poetic justice that this should happen right after he had announced he was going to leave me."

Katherine cleared her throat. "You should be told that it would be extremely unwise to go on like that with the police. What you are doing is showing what a powerful motive you had for pushing your husband into the harbor."

"Again," Diana said, looking Katherine directly in the eye.

Katherine nodded. "Precisely. Again. If there is any way to prove the first occurrence."

"The police have ways of finding the Pearsons," Emtee Dempsey said.

When Richard arrived, Kim was in her room upstairs and Joyce went to the door. Emtee Dempsey decided that this was not the time for Kim to confront her brother and Kim could not have agreed more. Nonetheless, she felt she was in hiding as she heard the sounds of voices lift from below. Richard was obviously trying to keep his under control. The presence of Katherine and Diana no doubt contributed to his ability to do so, but the sight of Kim could very well have been too much for him. The memory of his tour of the house earlier in the day would certainly return to haunt him. Kim wondered if Diana had felt like this during the day, a child concealing herself from the wrath of the grownups. Kim lay on her bed and stared at the ceiling. Joyce's supper plans were going to be completely bollixed up by all this commotion. She had assumed they would have one guest, Diana. Now they might have another, perhaps two, if Richard stayed. One thing Kim was sure of. She did not want to talk with her brother alone, not until he had lived down the rage he must be feeling.

There were steps on the stairway and she thought it must be Joyce. She was seated on the edge of her bed when Richard looked in. There was a smile on his face.

"They told me you weren't feeling well."

"I feel fine."

"So do I. This is the kind of cooperation I like. What got into Emtee Dempsey to call me right away like that?"

"Have you had a chance to talk with Diana yet?"

"Frawley's with me. She's taking down Mrs. Torrance's statement. At the harbor you mentioned the Pearsons. Why?"

"They were on the boat."

"What boat?"

"The Torrances' boat. Didn't Diana tell you?"

The benevolence that had so uncharacteristically been spread across Richard's face began to dissolve. Was he thinking that, for someone who was in her room indisposed, Kim seemed to know an awful lot about what Diana Torrance was telling Lucille Frawley?

"The Pearsons are in Florida," he said brusquely. They went to Sarasota a week ago."

Diana Moore Torrance's situation, already bad, went into steep decline from that point on. In the living room, no longer on his good behavior, Richard led them through their paces in a no-nonsense way Kim might have admired if she had not been, along with the others, in the dock. Even Katherine Senski submitted to Richard's authority with only a pro forma demur. When she invoked her status as a reporter, Richard just shook his head and pointed at the chair from which she had risen.

"You know the answer to that, Katherine. You're here as a friend on a social visit. Please spare me the constitutional crap. Sorry."

"Is a reporter ever really off duty, Lieutenant? Is an officer of the law?"

His expression made it clear that Katherine would be ill advised to pursue the thought that she and Richard were somehow on the same side.

The first thing Richard wanted clarified was Diana's presence in the house on Walton Street. Having made the easy assumption that she had shown up there shortly before he was called, he now wanted nothing left to surmise. So he was told of her visit some days before, to visit Sister Mary Teresa.

"About what?"

"A personal and private matter," Emtee Dempsey replied.

"What about?" Richard addressed the question a second time to Diana.

"I had some problems I wanted to discuss."

"Concerning your husband?"

Emtee Dempsey said, "You realize, Diana, you needn't answer any questions at all."

"But why shouldn't she?" Richard said sweetly. "Did your troubles concern your husband, Mrs. Torrance?"

"Yes."

"Were the two of you fighting, about to break up, what?"

Emtee Dempsey wanted to know why he would assume a thing like that.

"It has been mentioned," Richard said.

"Vivian Hoy?" Diana asked, her eyes flashing. She had taken a cigarette from a package and now seemed not to know what to do with it. Richard came and lit it for her. She looked up at him through a cloud of exhaled smoke. "Well?"

"Why would you think it would be Vivian Hoy?"

"Oh, for heaven's sake," Katherine said, "if you both answer questions with questions we'll be here forever."

Circuitously, mainly from Diana, but eventually from Kim as well, when Richard felt he finally understood the real purpose of her visit to Vivian Hoy that morning, the story of the star of the Chicago Brass came out.

"Your husband was having an affair with her?"

"I suppose you could call it that."

"And you wanted to make sure she was still alive," Richard said to Kim. "That's why you went there this morning, isn't it?"

"No, it isn't, Richard. I wanted to ask her if she could verify, if she would verify, what happened on the boat last night."

"And she refused."

"She lied," Diana said. "She says she was not on the boat at all last night."

"With you and your husband and the Pearsons?"

Kim could not warn Diana in time. "Yes. We were all there together. At least we were until I left."

"The Pearsons are in Florida, Mrs. Torrance."

If Kim had thought Vivian Hoy's look of surprise was feigned, Diana's seemed the soul of sincerity.

"But that's not possible."

A good deal that was not possible began to seem increasingly plausible. No significant element of Diana's account of what had happened the night before seemed to survive scrutiny. It was Sister Mary Teresa who first voiced the unthinkable.

"Richard, are you suggesting that Diana was responsible for her husband's death?"

"Put it this way, Sister. Every alternative she herself has put forward is as phony as a three-dollar bill. The Pearsons? Forget it. Vivian Hoy? Without the Pearsons, we have to accept her claim that she was never on the boat."

"Then by the same logic you must accept Mrs. Torrance's uncorroborated story. She says she was on the boat last night and left it. She returned to the harbor this morning to find that her husband had drowned. Very likely the victim of an accident," Emtee Dempsey added gratuitously.

"Ah, but the great difference, Sister Mary Teresa, is that Mrs. Torrance told us stories that are demonstrably false, whereas Vivian Hoy did not."

"Did she tell you she was chasing around with my husband?"

"I didn't say she made a general confession, Mrs. Torrance."

"She was on that boat last night, Lieutenant. She was on it when I went ashore."

"And the Pearsons were on it too?"

"Yes. I'm sure that was their name."

"You hadn't met them before?"

"No."

"Who identified them as the Pearsons?"

"Identified? It was an impromptu little party, Lieutenant. That is the name I thought Phil gave."

"You're not sure?"

Diana looked around at the others and in her eyes was the realization that she was losing credibility.

Emtee Dempsey said, "Pearsons, Smiths, what's in a name? What you must do, Richard, is find the couple who joined Diana and her husband and Miss Hoy on the boat last night. It will be someone anchored there in the marina."

"Who have not yet come forth," Richard said.

"Yes. I'm glad you noted that. It may very well be the most

significant thing to emerge from this otherwise dreary conversation."

Sister Mary Teresa pushed forward on her chair and then stood, as if giving the signal that she was dismissing them. Richard was apparently satisfied that he had learned all he was going to.

"Will you be staying here, Mrs. Torrance?" he asked from the doorway of the living room.

Diana looked around at the three nuns, but of course it was Sister Mary Teresa who answered.

"You are welcome to stay as long as you like, Diana. Richard, you yourself are welcome to stay for supper. I'm sure Sister Joyce has more than enough food for another guest."

It was fortunate for Emtee Dempsey's veracity and Joyce's hospitality that Richard was already overdue at home. Kim, who had watched Joyce's eyes cross at Emtee Dempsey's invitation, took Richard's arm before he might suggest phoning her sister-in-law. Katherine was company enough for Joyce without forewarning. Diana she had already known about, so there was a special meal of sorts on the way. Not that Joyce's ordinary fare would have been inadequate.

At table, Katherine asked Emtee Dempsey if she had been serious in suggesting that it was significant that the couple Diana had incorrectly identified as the Pearsons had not come forward. The old nun seemed about to take umbrage at the notion that anything she said might be wanting in seriousness, but she let it go by.

"Put yourself in their putative place, Katherine. You are invited on board a boat for a late-night drink by a man who is found drowned the following morning. Would not your instinctive reaction be to inform the authorities that you had been with the poor fellow only hours before his demise? Of course it would. When you add the occurrences Diana has told us of, it is incredible that the couple has not spoken up."

"Had you ever seen them before?" Katherine asked Diana.

"Yes, I think so. Oh, I wish I could be sure. Boat parties form and grow and subside in crazy ways. I often run into people who say they met me at some post-race celebration or whatever and I haven't the faintest idea who they are."

"Had you heard the name Pearson before?" The question was put by Joyce, a surprise in itself. She almost never took part in these speculative seminars.

"Oh, I must have."

"There is a Nelson who acts as agent for athletes."

"Tell me about Nelson the agent," Emtee Dempsey said.

Joyce seemed to know almost as much as Diana concerning the functions and activities of an agent; she was pretty well informed on Nelson too.

"He represented Vivian Hoy, didn't he?"

"He did indeed." There was an edge to Diana's voice.

Joyce said, "Vivian Hoy received the largest salary ever given a rookie soccer player when she turned professional."

"How long ago was that?" Emtee Dempsey asked.

"Five years," Diana said, as Joyce began to tick them off on her fingers.

"And how much was she paid to play football?"

When the sum was mentioned, Emtee Dempsey was not among those who looked stunned.

"Athletes have been receiving compensation worthy of their entertainment value in other sports for years. And why not? The profits from the contests are enormous. Why should not those who participate share in the spoils?"

"They take no risks. They have no overhead. They are not penalized when they play poorly." It was clear that Diana had further reasons, but Emtee Dempsey raised her hand.

"Let us stipulate that it is a moot matter. We do not want to get bogged down in a discussion of the pay given professional athletes. Vivian Hoy received a goodly amount of money and a man named Nelson played a role in her receiving it. Have you seen Nelson since he arranged matters for Vivian Hoy five years ago, Diana?"

"We renegotiated a year ago."

Joyce said, "Well, if I don't get these dishes done I may not get another contract."

That served as the cue for saying grace after meals, Emtee Dempsey deferring to Joyce's desire to clean up. Kim offered to help, so Emtee Dempsey took the two guests to her study.

"Do you believe her?" Joyce said after she had rinsed the dishes and put them in the washer. She held an unlit cigarette and looked at Kim with a little frown.

"Meaning you don't."

"Me? I don't know. I've never been in the kind of mess she's in. Losing her husband and in the way she did and then everybody wanting to know exactly what happened. Just when I seem to get a clear picture it goes vague."

Kim agreed, more or less. She was about to comment and then did not. The truth was that she was sick of the mysterious death of Philip Torrance. Her own day had been a shambles, beginning with the visit to Vivian Hoy. She had been made to look foolish, if not an outright liar; she had been scolded by Richard, and rightly so, after she had led him around by the nose. It would have been understandable if she were angry with Sister Mary Teresa, but Kim was too tired even for that.

She said her evening prayers alone, in the little chapel, and then went upstairs, got into pajamas, propped up her pillow, and settled down with the third volume of her condensed Gibbon. Within minutes she was sound asleep.

She was still propped up and the light burning when she awoke at one-thirty. It was surprising that the sound of her book hitting the floor had not brought someone to investigate. Kim turned off the light, settled into her bed, and lay sleepless. She agreed with Joyce. There was something untrustworthy about Diana and it was difficult to say what. No. It would have been difficult to say why she should be trusted. Did Emtee Dempsey believe her? Kim could not tell. In the morning, she would ask the old nun.

This promise to herself removed impediments to sleep and soon Kim was once more out of the world.

Four

The cut that ran over the four-times-weekly sports column of Norman Shire showed a smiling man with apple cheeks, a single brow, eyes nicely crinkled, and a full commanding mustache under the bulbous nose. The picture conveyed to the reader that here was a witty and reliable and above all knowledgeable source of sports news and information.

Once that had been true, but time had taken its toll not only on the visage depicted but on the moral fiber beneath. Norman had thought he wanted fame, recognition in restaurants and on the streets, recognition from his journalist peers, but when he had it, he realized it was not enough. Money? Money had always figured in his ambition, but it had come hand in hand with the fame, so it was not a separate target.

There are compensations other than professional ones, and

Norman sought fulfillment on the margin of his life as a sportswriter. He had married three times, always badly, but had the good luck to see his ex-wives go trekking off to the altar soon after they left him. Since there were no children — and sometimes in the wee hours Norman permitted himself to think that it was the absence of children that explained the painful hollowness in his guts — he had been relieved of all alimony claims. Katherine Senski, to whom he had confided, obliquely, ruefully, wittily, some version of his troubles, had suggested that having wearied of the world he was now ready for the consolations of religion. Maybe she was right. His own diagnosis was that what he had wanted all along was power.

Money and fame, he came to think, are only aspects of power. He actually read Nietzsche and, as he asked his mirror, how many sportswriters do you know who can spell Nietzsche, let alone truthfully claim to have read him? The alleged theoretician of Nazism awoke a resonance in the wizard of the *Tribune* sports page. The Will to Power. Did life finally come down to that, the urge to dominate, to put one's own imprint forcibly upon the world? If the theory was true, it did not point simply to the future, it should be a reasonable interpretation of his past life as well. And so he found it to be. By writing about sports he had come to control the destiny of those larger boys who had intimidated him on the playgrounds of his youth. The runty kid sent into right field when he was allowed to play at all or stuck in the goal at hockey, wanted not for any imagined skill at deflecting the puck but rather as a physical obstacle to its getting into the net, now as a man was feared. He made and broke reputations by tapping out a column. His handsome salary too was acknowledgment of his power.

But there remained a breed who, while vulnerable to his pen, was somehow independent still. The owner. The men and women who owned professional teams had a more direct and, if he could trust his discernment, more satisfying power over the players and also over the vast anonymous hordes of fans. Norman Shire resolved that he must, without losing the power he already had, acquire that wielded by the club owner. The combination of the two would put him in an unparalleled position.

To the jaundiced eye Philip Torrance might seem as improbable an entrepreneur as Norman Shire, but neither man was deceived about the quality of the other. Torrance saw through the remnants of the winning countenance that beamed out at his readers, not to the skull beneath the flesh but to the hard self-serving ambition that drove Shire. In Torrance Shire recognized a reasonable facsimile of his own thirst for more, ever more. Norman had known for years where Torrance's involvement in sports must necessarily lead. The only question was: would he have luck and money enough to achieve his goal? The luck looked to be less of a problem than the money, but Norman did not underestimate his man. His own nest egg, despite his disastrous marriages, continued to grow. He never saved less than twenty-five percent of what he earned and often managed to squirrel away more. His broker was a magician, more enthralled by the mathematics of the acquisition of wealth than money itself and thus largely trustworthy. Shire wanted to invest in a team, but he did not propose to be the principal owner. In fact, he aspired to anonymity. Real but anonymous power now seemed the most fulfilling dream. Keeping his ear to the ground and his eyes peeled, he swiftly put two and two together when he first saw Philip Torrance together with Eugene and Priscilla Evans. Given Evans's reputation as a financial shark — in again, out again, on to something else — he was a little surprised. When he saw them together a second time, he telephoned Torrance and said he would like to talk.

Had Torrance been less than Shire took him to be, the future owner of the Chicago Brass would have surmised that Norman

Shire was simply on the scent of a story. But from the moment they settled into canvas chairs on the deck of Torrance's boat, each man armed with a massive glass of bourbon on ice, a silent understanding was established. And Shire quickly made it audible.

"Are the Evanses going in with you?"

One blink of the eyes, a meditative sip of bourbon. "Off the record?"

"Off the record."

"It looks firm."

"Would you mind laying it out for me?"

"What is your interest?"

"I want in."

"How much do you know?"

"Enough to know I want in. Not nearly enough, however. It's a soccer team, right?"

"Women's soccer."

It was, he recognized afterward, a moment when the whole fabric of his life might have unraveled. He might have taken it to be a joke or, realizing that Torrance was serious, dismissed it as unserious. Had his expression changed at all? That was a question he had always wanted to put to Torrance. Now he would never be able to do that. Fortunately he had simply waited, and then Torrance was sketching it for him. He could come in for as low as five and as high as fifteen percent.

"I want twenty."

"I doubt that the others will agree."

"I don't give a damn about the others, Torrance. Look, with someone like Evans, you may need me around."

Torrance didn't come right out and agree with that but he said, "Okay. Why should I tell them twenty?"

"Because I will get us into Wrigley Field."

He got his twenty percent but it was not until the second

season that the Brass played in Wrigley Field. It was not their regular home grounds. The best Shire had been able to come through with was a once-monthly daytime home game at Wrigley Field. Torrance never let him forget it. The fact that they played the rest of the games in Comiskey did not matter nor the fact that they could play night games there. Torrance had been promised Wrigley Field and he did not have Wrigley Field. On the other hand, Norman Shire had his twenty percent. So far as he knew, the Evanses were happy enough with the site of the Brass home games. Shire despised Torrance for holding a grudge on such a silly point — the Brass were drawing crowds now no matter where they played — yet he also understood the tenacity with which his partner held him to the bargain he had made.

He had been guilty of hubris when he made the promise. The Will to Power does not always suffice. He made the Wrigley Field offer on the spur of the moment. At the time it seemed an inspiration. It also seemed one of those undoable feats one should occasionally hold oneself to perform. Well, he had not performed and the site of the Brass home games remained a bone of contention with Torrance even though neither of them had so much as mentioned it for half a year. Norman Shire had no delusion that Torrance would forgive and forget.

On the day Philip Torrance's body was found floating in Belmont Harbor, Katherine Senski came into his office at the *Tribune*, told him to be seated, and then gave him the news straight from the shoulder.

"When?" Norman Shire bleated.

"He was found this morning. He probably died last night."

Last night Norman had covered the Bradley game in Peoria. He almost said that aloud, as if he had to account for his whereabouts to Katherine.

"Is it on the wire or what?"

"Not yet. I got a phone call." It figured. The old doll had connections everywhere. "I knew you'd want to know."

How much did Katherine know about the Brass? One of his regrets was that he had not told her about his twenty percent interest in the club. When she found out from other sources — God knows what ones — Shire had admitted it without any fooling around, but he knew Katherine would have much preferred learning about it from him. He should know she did not use her knowledge unless she felt she had to. Did she mean to blow the whistle on him now? He guessed no.

"What do you want, Katherine?"

"The obvious. Is Torrance's death really a surprise? What has he been up to?"

He gave her everything on Torrance's philandering. As one who had himself sought happiness down that alley he had watched Torrance's antics with amusement and dismay and a little contempt. It didn't help that Norman liked Diana. A lot. She was his idea of a "class" woman. In his marrying days he might have made a play for her. Torrance should recognize what he had. Of course no husband did. Funny. Katherine apparently had heard nothing of Torrance's carryings on. Norman mentioned every woman he knew of except Vivian Hoy.

"How many irate husbands are there, for heaven's sake?"

"Maybe none. We live in altered times, Katherine."

"Not that altered. Your perspective has been skewed by your bad luck in marriage."

"I don't know about my perspective, but I sure was."

She snorted and sailed from his office. Shire remained at his desk, counting slowly to fifty. Then he rose, put on his jacket, strolled through the newsroom to the hallway where there was a cigarette machine. He bought a package of Camels. He had always smoked Camels. These were filtered, but they would have to do. He had not smoked for three years, seven months, and nineteen days. He lit up and inhaled deeply and very nearly blacked out. When his head cleared, he got into the elevator, went down and out and up the street to Finnegan's, where he ordered a shot of bourbon and a glass of beer. He had not had a drink for three years, seven months, and nineteen days. As soon as he got his bearings, he would phone Vivian.

When he telephoned there was no answer and he returned to the bar, had another boilermaker. The booze tasted better than the cigarettes. It was as though he had to make up as quickly as possible for all the smoking he had missed. He did not want to think of the agony it had cost him to quit. He had tried hypnotism, he had tried pills, he had even made a novena, but he could not get past breakfast without lighting up. So how had he simultaneously quit smoking and drinking the first time? Because his third wife said he couldn't. Where considerations of health and courtesy and self-respect had failed him, vanity carried the day. He could not tolerate some woman telling him he was too much a weakling to give up drinking and smoking. During the long months of abstinence he had regarded each day as thumbing his nose at Deborah. To hell with Deborah. She did not even realize what she had occasioned. He had seen her some months before and waited for her to comment on the fact that he was the only one in the room not smoking and drinking. Finally he had called her attention to it. She had been unimpressed. Well, would he give a damn if she told him she had quit smoking and drinking? Certainly not. The only person beside himself who would care that he had fallen off the wagon was Vivian Hoy.

He should not have made such a big deal of how much he used to drink and smoke when he told her about it, but of course he was trying to impress her. Already into his second drink and fourth cigarette, he felt as hooked as he had ever been. Those three years, seven months, and nineteen days now seemed unreal time, even wasted time. A sportswriter was meant to drink. It was part of the definition.

The problem was that he risked failing to achieve his ambitions when he drank. At the very least his ambition was tempered. On the other hand, would he have consolidated his position so far as the Chicago Brass was concerned if he had not been drinking at the time?

That was one of those questions to which we shall never know the answer, he informed himself. He decided it would be better to go over to Vivian's rather than telephone. She would need someone to talk to after the police had questioned her. It occurred to him that they would have as much reason or more to question him, once they learned of the twenty percent he held. And they would learn of it. He had imagined circumstances that would force the revelation of his partnership in the Brass, but he had never included the murder of Phil Torrance among the possibilities.

He had forgotten how the booze could alter the best-laid plans. On the way to Vivian's, he hit another bar — how many bars he had avoided during the past three years, seven months, and nineteen days! — and the taste for cigarettes returned with his next drink. He spent a good part of the day drinking, and when he was wakened by the sound of a telephone he did not know what day it was or, until he looked around, what bed he was in. It was a relief to find he was in his own bedroom. Alone. He picked up the phone, feeling almost like a solid citizen again.

"Mr. Shire, this is Sister Kimberly Moriarity. I wonder if you could spare me a few moments of your time."

"Did you say Sister?" His head, he realized, was aching. He wanted to ask his caller what day it was. Did she mean she was a nun?

That is what she meant. If Norman Shire had ever heard of the Order of Martha and Mary, he had forgotten it, but then he had tried to eradicate from hurtful memory most items from his Catholic upbringing. He was not sure how she conveyed the information that she was related to Lieutenant Richard Moriarity but this brought back sober apprehensions and it seemed the line of least resistance to agree to talk with her.

"At your office?"

His watch read eight-fifteen. "Come around nine. I'm just leaving."

"I didn't realize you worked nights."

Nights? Ye gods, was it nighttime? The drapes were pulled over his windows and he could not tell. But why would a nun lie?

He showered and shaved but felt little better than before. He wished he had corrected her and changed the appointment to nine tomorrow morning. The problem was, he did not know what tomorrow meant.

Kim had had some experience with the look of those who are becoming detoxified from alcohol. Her Uncle Willie had been an education in himself. One glance at Norman Shire — the waxen skin, the way he moved his hands — told her he was still under the waning influence of the alcohol he had consumed. It lessened her apprehension at seeing a legend in flesh and blood. She had been assured by Joyce that he was a legend.

"Then come on in with me and talk to him."

"Oh no you don't. I'll wait here in the car. Just go up there and grill him good. Where were you on the night Phil Torrance got dumped in the lake? That sort of thing. It'll break the ice."

"Ha ha."

But that was pretty much what Emtee Dempsey expected her to do with Norman Shire. Ever since Katherine had divulged the sportswriter's partial ownership of the Chicago Brass, the old nun had been itching to talk to him. The fact that he seemed to have disappeared right after Katherine told him what had happened to Torrance made her all the more eager. When Kim reached him by phone tonight she had not for a moment dreamed he would tell her to come right over to his *Tribune* office. A copy of the most recent issue of the paper was spread open on his desk when she came in. Was he trying to catch up on the world? His name was mentioned in the story on the Torrance murder.

"I suppose the police have been pestering you about that?" Kim indicated the paper.

"Poor Phil," Norman Shire said.

"You're no longer a silent partner."

"It doesn't matter," he said, but he didn't seem to think she would believe him. "Not much here about Diana."

"What do you mean?"

"Isn't she a suspect?"

"I understand it is Vivian Hoy the police are most interested in."

Kim did not exactly cross her fingers when she said this. It was her principal instruction from Emtee Dempsey, who had been primed by Katherine Senski. She was particularly instructed to report his reaction to the remark.

He rubbed his eyes and when he looked at her they seemed not to be focusing properly. She was not sure he had heard what she had said.

"Vivian Hoy," she began, but he showed her a palm.

"I heard you. You said on the phone you're a nun."

"That's right."

"You don't look like a nun."

"Few nuns do anymore. We've changed."

"Why?"

"Would we be having this conversation if I were wearing one of the old habits?"

"Why not? I always talked to nuns in the old days. You're the first one like you I've talked to."

"So far as you know. We don't advertise our religious profession."

"I don't get it."

Well, not everybody did. Sister Mary Teresa did not. She thought it utter foolishness for the daughters of Blessed Abigail Keineswegs, the foundress of the Order of Martha and Mary, to be dressing like other women in order to engage in allegedly more meaningful work. Emtee Dempsey did not know what work could be more meaningful than the education of young women. Nor did she need to get rid of her wimple and veil in order to excel as a woman. She had an international reputation as a medieval historian and she had gained it dressed as a nun should dress. Her correspondents were scattered throughout the world. Without leaving the cloister she had made her influence felt in Chicago, in the country, in the world. She thought it ludicrous that grown women should believe that a change of clothing and address would make them more effective witnesses in the world.

Norman Shire's nonreaction to the mention of Vivian Hoy was what she would have to report to the old nun. Or would have had to if the remark had not finally penetrated the reporter's mind. His eyes managed to focus and he stared at her.

"Vivian! My God, no." His hand went groping for his telephone. "I tried to call her," he said, apparently to Kim, perhaps to the world at large.

"Would you like me to dial it?"

He glared at her. "I can do it."

"I only meant I suppose you usually have a secretary to place your calls for you."

This placated him. He pushed an address book across the desk toward her, along with the phone. He opened his desk and came forth with a bottle of aspirin.

"Dial her number while I take a couple of these."

He left the office and Kim punched the numbers written next to Vivian in the book. Just Vivian. But the book was divided by letters and she was under H. After she finished dialing, Kim pressed the phone to her ear and waited.

The phone was still ringing in her ear when he came back into the office. He took it from her, listened for a time, then hung it up.

"Will you go over there with me?"

"Why would you want me along?"

"I'm worried. Look, I called her yesterday." He hesitated, seemed about to add something, then didn't. "No one answered so I hung up. I should have gone over there before."

"I have someone waiting for me downstairs. Another nun. She is a fan of yours."

Even in these trying circumstances he could not be indifferent to that.

"You say she's a nun?"

"Joyce. She knows more about sports than anyone I know. That doesn't sound like much, I realize."

"She reads my column, eh?" He seemed to suggest that this would be the explanation of Joyce's knowledge.

"Religiously," Kim said.

He glanced at her. They had come into the hallway where he had punched the elevator button. "I'll overlook that."

Joyce sat behind the wheel of the VW bug, gripping it as they came along the walk toward her. Kim brought Norman Shire to the window of the driver's seat, the better to introduce him to his fan. Joyce handled it well.

"You look different in black and white."

"I have a headache."

Kim said, "We're going to take Mr. Shire to Vivian Hoy's apartment." They got into the car and Joyce looked openmouthed at Kim.

"Repeat what you said."

"We're going to call on Vivian Hoy."

"I don't believe it."

"If she's home." Shire spoke from the back seat, where he seemed to be sitting sidesaddle. His head was scrunched into his shoulders.

"Mainly I want to check and see if she's home."

"She's not home," Joyce said.

"How do you know that?"

"There's a game tonight."

Shire slapped his forehead with his palm. "Ladies, be my guest. I'll take you to the game."

Joyce had the motor running before he finished. She pulled away from the curb and headed in the direction of White Sox Park.

Nothing is easier than to be a snob about a sport one doesn't understand. Kim watched the players move up and down on the field below, and each time there was a roar from the crowd she tried to see what it was that elicited the response; but she never could, except, of course, when someone attempted a goal — and that seemed very seldom. So she settled for enjoying the pageantry spread out below them as they looked on from the press box. Norman Shire had had a restorative beer and was now drinking coffee and seemed much better.

"Which one is Vivian Hoy?" Kim asked, and Joyce had said that her number was 16. "Where is she?"

"I don't see her," Joyce said.

It turned out she was not playing. When this became clear, Norman Shire lost interest in the game.

"I'll go downstairs and check."

It was the last they saw of him. Joyce was absorbed in the game and Kim did not have the heart to suggest they leave. So they stayed for the entire game. Only when it was over did Joyce react to Norman Shire's absence.

"Coming was his idea," she said, as if Kim meant to scold her.

"No doubt he went to find Vivian Hoy. She never did play, did she?"

"I would have told you, Kim."

They found their car in the parking lot and slowly exited,

not making much progress until they got to the outer drive. Kim wondered what she had of interest to report to Emtee Dempsey. She wouldn't be surprised if the old nun had already gone to bed. It was nearly eleven o'clock.

When they arrived at Walton Street it was clear that no one had retired. The first floor was ablaze with light and half the windows on the second floor were also lit up.

"What on earth is going on?" Kim said when Joyce pulled into the curb. She skipped up the steps and opened the front door to confront her brother Richard.

"Where in hell have you been?"

"I beg your pardon?"

"Sister Mary Teresa refused to tell me where you were."

"Why should she tell you?"

Kim started past him but he took hold of her arm — firmly, but not too firmly.

"Kim, this is serious. You were at Vivian Hoy's apartment yesterday, weren't you?"

"I already told you I was."

"'Admitted you were' would be more like it. I have to take you down for questioning. It would look bad if I didn't."

"Is it a crime to pay a visit on Vivian Hoy?"

"Haven't you heard?"

What Kim heard was the familiar thump of Emtee Dempsey's cane coming along the hallway.

"Richard, you can speak with your sister right here. There is no need in the world to take her away."

"What happened?" Kim asked.

Emtee Dempsey answered. "Vivian Hoy is dead."

"Oh, my God."

It was Joyce who spoke. She had come in behind Kim and they turned to look at her. She put out her hand, seeking support from the wall, and then slumped to the floor.

The next few moments were chaos. Kim, to her immense self-disgust, let out a wail as Joyce slid to the floor, her eyes rolling upward into her head. Richard said something profane and helpless. It was Emtee Dempsey who barged through and got behind Joyce, lifting her and almost immediately being helped by Diana Torrance, who had followed Emtee Dempsey down the hall. Diana seemed to know exactly what she was doing as she put her hands beneath Joyce's arms and eased her to a sitting position.

"Get a glass of water," she said to Richard, and he disappeared in the direction of the kitchen looking considerably relieved to have something to do. Joyce's eyes fluttered open.

"She's had altogether too much excitement," Emtee Dempsey said.

"We went to the Brass game," Kim said.

"Exactly."

Richard came with the water, Joyce was revived and, embarrassed, got to her feet, shrugging off all further efforts of help.

"I'm all right. I've never fainted in my life." She might have been swearing the rest of them to secrecy.

Diana insisted on helping Joyce upstairs and then, in a way that just happened, Emtee Dempsey, Kim, and Richard were seated in the study. The old nun had detoured past the kitchen and picked up a beer for Richard and he settled down with it as if he had forgotten all about wanting to take Kim downtown for questioning.

"Is Vivian Hoy really dead?" Kim asked.

"She was found in her apartment this afternoon. She missed a practice and when she couldn't be raised on the telephone one of the players went over there and found the body."

"It's odd they didn't mention that at the game."

"No, it isn't. Can you imagine that? 'Ladies and gentlemen, it is our pleasure to inform you that the star of the Chicago Brass was found dead in her apartment this afternoon. Foul play is suspected.' Not very likely, Kim."

Kim turned to Emtee Dempsey. "Was Diana here?"

"At the time of the murder? Don't pussyfoot about, Sister Kimberly. When was the time of death, Richard?"

"Approximately dawn. Say between four and seven this morning."

Emtee Dempsey wrinkled her nose. "I suppose Diana could have slipped out and killed her. I got up at six and Joyce and I went to the cathedral for seven-o'clock Mass. I certainly didn't check to see if Diana was in her room. Perhaps Joyce did."

"Good Lord, you're not much help," Kim said.

"If she did it I would not want it to go undiscovered. Is Diana Torrance one of your suspects, Richard?"

"I assume you're just kidding around and that she was here at the time Vivian Hoy died. The one we have the call out for is Norman Shire. Since Kim was seen with him at the *Tribune* office, I assumed you had brought him here. This is the first place I look for people now."

"Now you are kidding," Emtee Dempsey said, but there was a little throb of delight in her voice.

"He took Joyce and me to the game."

"Uh huh."

"He did!"

"Where did you sit?"

"In the press box."

Richard frowned. "Then why didn't we find him there?"

"He left as soon as he saw that Vivian wasn't playing. He said he was going to her apartment."

"Well, he must not have gotten there. He would have been picked up as soon as he showed his face within a mile of that place."

The phone on Sister Mary Teresa's desk began to ring. The

old nun let Kim take it, since she never answered the phone if it were physically possible for someone else to do so. The call was for Richard. His eyes moved back and forth from Kim to Emtee Dempsey as he listened. He began to stand up, still saying nothing. He ws nodding as if his caller could see him. "I'll be right down," he said finally. "Read him his rights, let him call a lawyer, don't talk to him. I want first shot at him."

He hung up the phone and pushed it back across the desk.

"Good news?" Emtee Dempsey asked.

"They picked up Norman Shire as he entered Vivian Hoy's building. Of course he doesn't know that she is dead."

"Richard, I can't believe he did. He was genuinely surprised she wasn't playing. He told us he was going to see about it."

"When was that?"

"At the game."

"I mean, how long ago?"

"Not two hours ago."

"What took him so long to get to Vivian Hoy's apartment from White Sox Park?"

Richard left that question lying on Emtee Dempsey's desk, so to speak, and, having drained his beer, was on his way. The two nuns sat in silence. Emtee Dempsey broke it.

"Tell me all about Norman Shire."

"There is very little to tell."

"That is why I want it all."

She wanted a good deal more than Kim could supply and ultimately had recourse to Katherine Senski.

"Do you realize what time it is?" Katherine said when, after eight rings, she answered her phone.

"Eleven-thirty. Needless to say, I am calling for Sister Mary Teresa."

"Needless to say."

What Emtee Dempsey learned from that phone call and

had supplemented by later inquiries bore on Norman Shire's checkered career: success professionally, failure personally. Of course the most tantalizing bit of information was his twenty-percent ownership of the Chicago Brass.

"He is also sweet on Vivian Hoy. Or was. And I think he was susceptible to Mrs. Torrance as well. The man simply could not learn, where women are concerned."

Diana and Joyce looked in while the phone conversation was in progress and Emtee Dempsey waved them in. She covered the receiver with her hand and whispered "ice cream" to Joyce. Her idea of the ultimate late-night treat was a chocolate sundae, and when she ate a sundae everyone ate a sundae. Moreover, given what Katherine had just told her on the phone, she realized she had beneath her roof another source of information on Norman Shire.

Of course, she had asked Diana about her business partner after Katherine put them on to the sportswriter, and the response had been fairly bland. Now, over chocolate sundaes in Emtee Dempsey's study, Diana was more circumstantial.

"He had a terrible drinking problem at one time. I suppose there were years when he wasn't really sober from January to December. For the most part it didn't interfere with his work. Certainly his status as sportswriter has always been high."

"He's the best," Joyce said, but she might have been influenced by Norman Shire's role in getting her a seat in the press box for that night's game.

Five

The biggest event of the next two days was the funeral Mass for Philip Torrance. Sister Mary Teresa, cast willy-nilly into the role of confidante and mainstay of the widow, did not hesitate to accept Diana's invitation to sit in the first pew with her. And, ever a stickler for the customs of yesteryear, Emtee Dempsey needed a sister in religion to accompany her on any excursion into the wicked world. Perhaps Kim was predestined to be chosen anyway, but Joyce, just to be on the safe side, began to cough theatrically at every opportunity once the danger was clear.

"Maybe you should quit smoking," Kim suggested when they were alone in the kitchen.

"Kim, I hate funerals."

"I'm not exactly dying to go to one myself."

"Funny. Anyway, Emtee Dempsey prefers you."

Teacher's pet? Maybe. Kim supposed that the old nun did look on her with a species of favor. Before the Order disintegrated, Sister Mary Teresa had seen young Sister Kimberly as her heir apparent. Now there was no throne to occupy, but Kim still worked on her doctorate in history at Northwestern. When it did not interfere with other errands, that is, like accompanying Emtee Dempsey to the funeral of the husband of another former student.

Kim could not guess what the old nun made of Diana Moore Torrance. Did she believe a word the woman had told her? It would be difficult to imagine a story with more holes in it than the one Diana had brought to Walton Street. Although it could be proven that the Torrances owned a boat, there was nothing other than Diana's word for the fact that they had been on it the night her husband died. Indeed, her claim that Vivian Hoy and the Pearsons had been with them had conflicted with what Vivian herself had told Kim. And now Vivian too was dead, her body found in that wonderful apartment Kim had visited. All Richard would tell her was what he was telling the papers: death did not seem to have been due to natural causes. In any case, Vivian could no longer deny or confirm Diana's story. As for the Pearsons, it seemed physically impossible for them to have been on the Torrance boat at anchor in Belmont Harbor while at the same time occupying their condominium in Sarasota.

"But, Sister Kimberly, if we are to doubt her, let us be thorough about it. We have only her word about that night on the boat, yes. That is true. If we doubt it, we no longer have an ostensible motive, namely that her husband publicly humiliated her and, after years of womanizing, informed Diana that he was leaving her. Furthermore, she is no longer to be thought of as having knocked him into the water and saying before witnesses that she wished he had drowned. There are no witnesses."

"So what on earth do you make of it?"

"Sister, Sister, isn't that obvious? Why did she go to such extremes to put herself in a bad light? Why does she want me, and you, to suspect her of killing her husband?"

Having said that, Emtee Dempsey had turned away, determined to produce her daily quota of pages, no matter these exciting distractions and unusual demands on her time. Kim was left to ponder on her own the implications of the possibility that nothing Diana had told them was true and that she was thereby beyond suspicion. Was she deflecting attention from someone else? Such tempting hypotheses, which, after all, were the reward of Emtee Dempsey's involving them in affairs best left to the police, became suddenly irrelevant when the body of Vivian Hoy had been found and attention turned to Norman Shire.

On the day preceding the funeral, Emtee Dempsey had kept after Kim to invite Richard to Walton Street so that they could find out what the police really thought of Norman Shire as a murder suspect. It was a lot easier to find what Katherine Senski thought.

"Total and absolute and preposterous rubbish, Sister Mary Teresa," the veteran reporter said.

She said it on the phone and she repeated it in Emtee Dempsey's study when she swung past the house on Walton Street on the way to her apartment from the offices of the *Tribune*. Kim had the persistent thought of Arabs folding their tents whenever Katherine swept into the house. Seated across from Sister Mary Teresa, enjoying a cigarette and the sauterne Joyce had poured for her, Katherine was clearly angry at as well as loyal to her colleague on the *Tribune*.

"Well, for one thing, he's a man. That means he's foolish, vain, talkative, and an absolute ass when it comes to women. He can't tolerate this either." Katherine flourished her glass.

"He is against drinking?"

"It's the other way around. He is an alcoholic, whatever that is. He can't drink, that's for sure. He stopped drinking years ago."

"Apparently he started again," Emtee Dempsey said softly. Her tone seemed a concession to Katherine's feeling, but it was also obvious that she was dissatisfied with Katherine's inference. The qualities she had attributed to Norman Shire suggested amorous activity. Was this Katherine's meaning? "Of course he was in love with Vivian Hoy. He was half in love with me, for heaven's sake." Katherine laughed, but she laughed alone. Emtee Dempsey closed her eyes.

"'Half in love with easeful Death.'" Her eyes popped open and she stared at Kim. "Who wrote that?"

"Keats."

"That's right. Poets never lie. It is a possible human emotion, a dreamy wish to be no more. There are forms of suicide that are not necessarily fatal."

"Are you talking about Vivian Hoy?" Katherine asked, somewhat impatiently. Had she wanted the conversation to dwell for a moment on a younger man's hankering for her? Emtee Dempsey sat forward.

"Have you heard something?" Katherine had heard nothing about an official verdict on Vivian Hoy's death. So Norman Shire again became the topic. "Here is an alcoholic, a man with endless affairs with women, aging now, no doubt, who kills two people and..."

"Two people!" Katherine nearly spilled her drink.

"Philip Torrance makes one and Vivian Hoy makes two. He was a business partner of his first victim. What was going wrong with that football team, Katherine? What kind of falling-out had there been?"

"Sister Mary Teresa, you cannot take real people and just dream up exciting stories about them. I heard of nothing but success so far as the Chicago Brass are concerned. In just a few years it had become one of the genuine successes in women's soccer."

"But that was Philip Torrance's doing, wasn't it?"

"And his wife's."

"Exactly. What did Norman Shire have to do with that success?"

"More than the Evanses, I imagine, but not really much."

"Ah, the Evanses."

They were not to meet the Evanses until the funeral. Sister Mary Teresa, resplendent in the habit the Blessed Abigail Keineswegs had designed for her spiritual daughters some centuries before, was not an easily ignorable person at the funeral of Philip Torrance. The fact that she followed the casket up the aisle at Diana's side, eschewing her cane for the occasion (even so, it would have been hard to say who was leaning on whom), all but made her the center of attraction. The picture that appeared in the *Tribune* was taken when the two women were in the aisle. The *Sun-Times* ran an art shot, the two front rows of mourners in profile, the faces seeming to fuse into one. The mayor, a background figure in the *Trib*'s picture, was as prominent as anyone else in the *Sun-Times*. The Evanses were in the same pew as Kim, just behind Diana and Emtee Dempsey. They were in their early- to mid-sixties, affluent-looking, silver-haired, he with a complementary mustache. If there was the slightest unease in their manner, it might have had to do with the way the reminder of mortality mocks the successes of this world. That and a general unfamiliarity with what went on in churches in even the best of circumstances. Mrs. Evans kept her arm firmly in her husband's, and her serene, half-amused smile seemed to Kim more habitual than real. His silver brows met in an almost-frown and his expression seemed to say that something would have to be done about people dying. Kim could imagine him as chairman of the local campaign, soliciting funds so that medical science could make a major effort to solve the problem.

The undertaker had greeted Kim quizzically and she should have known in advance that he was the kind of Catholic who would react hostilely to the news that she was a nun. His name was McDivitt and his professional look of sorrow comported ill with his ruddy, rounded countenance.

"Sister as in nun?" McDivitt was over fifty and thus would have a notion of nuns that went well with Emtee Dempsey. He had fallen over himself being deferential to the old nun. That is when Kim had become separated from her alleged companion.

"I am Sister Mary Teresa's companion," Kim said as sweetly as she could.

"Ah, you're a nurse."

Kim let it go. She hated moments like this. It had been the same way at Vivian Hoy's when the athlete learned she was a nun. It made Kim feel like an imposter. Of course, with Vivian that is what she had been. If only on his own terms, McDivitt had accepted her as a member of the inner circle of mourners and thus she had ended up with the Evanses in the second pew.

"I've never been to a Catholic funeral," Mrs. Evans whispered, and her tone seemed to invite some secret handshake of shared puzzlement. Mr. Evans stared at Kim noncommittally over his wife's shoulder. He looked as Kim supposed someone worth seven million dollars might look.

"It's really not that different," Kim said enigmatically. The Evanses looked at her as if she had failed some test.

That Evans was worth seven million dollars was one of the facts about him they had gleaned from the materials Katherine Senski had sent over from the *Tribune*. Eugene Evans was a native of Manchester, New Hampshire, who had inherited money from a family mill, gone to Williams College, spent the war years in OSS with Wild Bill Donovan, and ever since devoted himself to making his money grow steadily. He had moved to Chicago when the Kennedys owned the Merchandise Mart and had stayed on. He was considered a gentleman buccaneer by those who had not been harmed by his dealing. Mrs. Evans, Priscilla, had gone to Smith. They had met in New York after the war when she was taking a halfhearted fling at being a career girl. She retired with relief when she married Eugene. Their only child, a son, was severely retarded and had been under expensive private care almost from birth. The Evanses had coped with that problem, as generally they coped with problems, by buying a solution to it. Neither of them had seen their son since he was eighteen months old, when they faced the fact that he was incurably retarded. All this had come out, along with a pathetic picture of the child, now in his thirties, in a gossipy exposé that had been published in a minor scandal sheet because the Evanses did not qualify for such big-league slander as the *National Inquirer*. No one would have guessed this tragic dimension in their lives by looking at the Evanses. The stoic mien seemed so obviously a façade that Kim felt her heart go out to the couple.

Eugene Evans's financial career, to the degree Kim could understand it, seemed a matter of sedate gambling, moving money around like chips, collecting his winnings, moving on, while all along paying as few taxes as were legally required. The Chicago Brass seemed a departure from the pattern of Evans's investment.

"Was he a friend of Torrance?" Emtee Dempsey wanted to know.

"You have everything there," Katherine said, indicating the photocopies of the *Tribune* material. It made an impressive mountain on Sister Teresa's desk. As usual, the old nun sought the meaning of events in documents, certain they would provide the solution to the death of Philip Torrance as well as that of Vivian Hoy.

"Maybe they'll give us a cure for cancer too," Joyce muttered cynically in the kitchen afterward.

Diana's attitude toward the Evanses had been difficult to decipher. That was one of the chief tasks Emtee Dempsey had assigned Kim. She wanted to know how the remaining owners of the Chicago Brass behaved toward one another. The older couple were awkward in expressing their sympathy, but there was scarcely anything significant in that. Who other than a priest or a mortician handles such situations with ease?

The Mass was in the Torrances' parish church, the celebrant one of the assistant pastors; clearly neither Philip nor Diana had made much of an impression there and the notoriety of Phil Torrance in death changed nothing. The homily was blessedly general, no forced eulogy of the deceased, rather a reminder to those in the pews that their lives too must one day end. Perhaps today. The priest, bald and obese, did not try for rhetorical flourish. The fact that any of them might fall dead in his tracks in the course of the day was just that, a fact. No reference at all was made to the fact that Phil Torrance had apparently been pushed. It would not have altered the point of the sermon.

The façade of the Evanses' sophistication cracked when they were at the cemetery, a small group gathered around a casket suspended over its freshly dug grave. All eyes were pulled downward. It was like a scene in *Hamlet*. Not that Kim was unaffected herself. Far from it. The mark of the shovel was visible on the walls of the grave, and at its bottom was the concrete vault into which the casket would go. The priest read matter-of-factly from a book, the breeze rippling its pages, and Diana began to weep. Emtee Dempsey, headdress picking up the breeze like a spinnaker, hugged her old student close. Kim did not think the tears hypocritical. It was impossible not to feel grief in such circumstances. She felt that she could weep for a stranger just then. Despite all the troubles the Torrance marriage had known, they had, after all, been man and wife for twenty years. Priscilla's stiff upper lip visibly trembled and Eugene blinked his eyes rapidly several times and then sought something on the horizon that could get him through these awful moments. When it was over, they moved swiftly back to the road where the cars were parked. Kim, mindful of her mission from Emtee Dempsey, hurried after them. The four limousines had been hired by Evans to carry the auxiliary party, a gun-metal blue fleet to contrast with the single McDivitt Cadillac in which Diana and Emtee Dempsey had ridden. It was Evans too who had laid on the brunch at the Hilton. At the moment he seemed to be regretting having gotten so far involved in such distasteful rites.

"For God's sake, cremate me when I die," he said to his wife. "I don't want to put people through this sort of thing."

She shivered. "Don't even talk about it." She smiled at Kim, another invitation to join the inner circle, the real people. Kim raised her brows and sighed. It was the best she could do.

If the funeral and burial were depressing, the brunch at the Hilton soon took on a festive air. The general tone of the gathering stemmed from the majority of sports-related people there. The open bar helped to get everyone into a happier mood and Evans, though he did not himself drink, smiled over his glass of orange juice at his guests as if he had just saved them from the grave itself. Kim's glass of orange juice seemed to attract his. He came to stand beside her.

"Do you know many of these people?"

Katherine Senski was there, of course, but what Kim had noticed was the number of police scattered through the crowd. She found it hard to believe that anyone interested in their possible presence would not recognize them, they seemed so obvious to her. From the bar, Richard looked across the intervening heads at Kim and Evans. "Only a few."

"You really are a nun?" He tipped his head slightly to one side and a little smile played on his lips. She could confide in him.

"Yes. Sister Mary Teresa and I are members of the Order of Martha and Mary."

"But she has on that elaborate get-up, whereas you..." He considered Kim's suit and shrugged.

"Come. I'll introduce you to her."

"Oh, I don't think so." He looked alarmed.

"You'll like her. People do."

This was borne out by the small crowd that had gathered round the chair in which Emtee Dempsey had sat as soon as she arrived at the hotel. She would never admit to being tired, but Kim knew she must be exhausted. Evans was looking around for a gracious way out of this. Kim put her hand firmly on his elbow and steered him in the direction of the little crowd. Let Emtee Dempsey figure out Eugene Evans. To Kim he remained opaque.

Any notion that Emtee Dempsey had put aside the curiosity that had prompted her to tell Kim to keep an eye on Evans was dispelled when she spied Kim approaching and immediately, like Canute commanding the waves, though with better effect, cleared a path for them with an imperious gesture. Evans could have been forgiven if he felt he was being granted an audience.

"Sister Kimberly, I want to meet your friend."

Evans was clearly pleased. And he was relieved, too, that the old nun did not threaten some social gaucherie. Within minutes he and Emtee Dempsey were deep in conversation alone, the rest dispersed. Kim went to the bar where Richard was still at his post. A drink was at his elbow.

"Better watch that," Kim warned. They had uncles who drank to excess and both considered problem drinking a possibly inherited trait. Their mother had gotten into the habit of warning them about drink and each of them had taken it up with the other.

"What were you talking with Evans about?"

"I was identifying the policemen in the room for him."

"Funny."

"I skipped you. This is your chance to win a citation."

"The widow seems to have recovered." Diana was drinking a Bloody Mary from which an enormous stalk of celery sprouted. It did not seem to be her first.

"She's been through a lot."

"Poor little rich girl."

Diana *was* rich, when you stopped to think of it. But then, she had been rich for years. It had not made her happy, certainly.

Kim said, "Have you found the couple that was on the Torrance boat with Vivian Hoy and Diana the night Philip Torrance drowned?"

He looked at her. "How did you know?" he asked, disgust on his voice.

"I thought the Pearsons were in Florida."

They *had* flown to Sarasota a week before the death of Philip Torrance, that much was true. But George Pearson had returned to the city on a flying visit and taken a girl he picked up out to his boat for a party. They had joined Torrance and his girl friend and wife and things had occurred pretty much as Diana said they had.

"Pearson told you this?"

"The girl. Wilma. She is one of those kids who hang around the harbor, crew for various boats, party a lot. She figured she ought to tell us what she knew. Pearson corroborates it, reluctantly. He would like to wring her neck."

"So Diana was telling the truth. Maybe that's why it sounded so funny."

"You sound relieved."

Kim picked up Richard's glass, took a sip, managed not to gag. "Not really. I mean, if she had nothing to do with Vivian Hoy's death..."

"If that is Emtee Dempsey's reasoning, tell her to go back to square one. Torrance was very probably murdered."

"What about Vivian Hoy's death?"

"She talked to Gleason and O'Connell. Very edgy girl. There was lots of booze in her apartment and we found cocaine as well."

"Suicide?"

"That seems to be the indication."

"What about Norman Shire?"

"There he is."

The sportswriter had not been in evidence at the church or cemetery but there he was indeed, leaning against the wall, alone, looking with vacant eyes at the people who had come to eat and drink in memory of Philip Torrance. His expression was that of a man who had come back from something more harrowing than a religious rite for the deceased. He had the look of a man who has utterly lost his self-esteem. A waiter stopped to take his order and Shire shook his head impatiently. But before the waiter got away, he grabbed his arm and muttered something. He wore a look of despair. Then he fumbled in his pocket and brought out a package of cigarettes. What dreadful moral drama was being enacted on the margins of this now joyful gathering?

"I'll say hello," Kim said.

Shire saw her when she was half across the room. He pushed away from the wall and might have fled if the waiter had not come with his drink. He took it carefully from the tray. Don't spill. Kim came up to him and raised her orange juice.

"Cheers."

He looked at her and then her glass. He raised his in a toast. "When I think of all the juice I drank."

"It's good for you."

"Is it? And these may be dangerous to your health?" He flourished his cigarette, then put it to his mouth and took an enormous drag, inhaling the smoke as deeply as he could. "I wonder why the hell I wanted to live a long life."

"Are you so ready for the next one?"

"Tell me about the next life, Sister. That's your job, isn't it?"

"Oh, I have a few concerns in this one. Like how did Vivian Hoy meet her death."

"I killed her." If this was a macabre joke, Shire's expression gave no clue of it. "I don't expect you to believe me. The police don't believe me either. Well, why should they assume my burden? It isn't as if I remember doing it." He drank. One hand brought the glass to his mouth, and a moment later the other brought the cigarette. Kim had the idea that the two motions could be timed and there would be a very exact interval between them.

"Why are we standing?" she asked.

"I'm standing because I haven't fallen down. That will come later."

"We'll be eating shortly."

"Not I. I am, in the phrase, putting in an appearance. When the others go in to eat, I shall adjourn to the bar."

"You shouldn't."

"A nun shouldn't be talking to an old sinner either."

"If that were true, nuns would have no one to talk to. Including one another. If you go to the bar, I'll come with you."

He shrugged. "Suit yourself. They have lots of juice."

He had two more drinks before the waiters began to circulate among the now animated crowd announcing that food would soon be served and they should take their places at the tables. Shire handed his glass to the third waiter who told them this and said to Kim, "I'm going."

They went together out of the banquet room into a hall where they had a choice of eight elevators. The bar was below street level, a dim place that never saw the sun.

"There is only one time in bars," Shire said, when Kim

mentioned this. "Drinking time. Are you sticking with orange juice or will I corrupt you too?"

"Too?"

"That is the story you have come to listen to, my dear."

"I'll have orange juice."

"Good girl."

He stayed with Scotch. And cigarettes. It was called chain smoking. He was a chain drinker too, shackled to his habits, a willing if not happy slave.

"So what's the long story?" Kim asked.

He closed his eyes. "Now each man kills the thing he loves. . ." His memory failed him for a moment. "The coward does it with a kiss, the brave man with a sword." He opened his eyes. "Cowards can kill with swords too, but I suppose the kiss is still applicable."

When he fell off the wagon three days and — he glanced at his watch — four hours and twenty minutes ago — he had sunk swiftly into the zombie-like trance that enables one who is all but completely drunk to pass among the sober undetected. His last conscious memory was of setting off to see Vivian Hoy. He woke in his bed more than twenty-four hours later. "To answer the phone and hear for the first time thy dulcet cloistered voice, my dear. I had no idea whether it was day or night. That is why I made the appointment for nine, thinking it must be morning. When we talked she was already dead."

"Yes, and you were as unaware of that as I was."

"That means nothing. The essence of thorough drunkenness is that one goes on saying and doing things of which later he has not the least memory. Maybe sleepwalking is like that. It is spooky the first time you realize you have been moving about in the world, crossing streets, talking to people, doing everything, and in total unconsciousness. At least, what is done in that condition never hooks up in memory with conscious life."

"And you maintain that you killed Vivian Hoy while you were in such a condition?"

He frowned. "Well, I would have led up to it more dramatically, but that is it in a nutshell. I see you look dubious."

"Doubtful. Along with the police, and that is decisive. No matter how unaware you might have been, you would have left a trace of yourself. If there had been anything in Vivian Hoy's apartment to connect you with her death, you wouldn't be free to drink yourself into oblivion again."

"But there is something."

"What?"

"My booze. When I swore off the stuff, Viv offered to take it and give it a home. Perhaps she thought I could never stick to my resolution. I guess she was right, eventually. Three years, seven months, and nineteen days after I went cold turkey, I was back on the sauce. I suppose that was my real reason for going to her apartment. I was a bad influence on her, by the way. She had never smoked before she met me. Imagine, an athlete taking up smoking while at the height of her powers. As an owner of the Brass I should have objected. As someone who loved Vivian I should have objected. But I took a perverse satisfaction in seeing her smoke. And drink. I suppose that is the only pleasure a devil gets, leading others into misery."

"Cocaine was found in her apartment too."

He was quite genuinely shocked. He shook his head. "No. No, she wouldn't get mixed up with that. How would you know, anyway?"

"The police..."

His eyes narrowed. "That's right. Your brother the cop. Did he tell you that?"

"A combination of alcohol and drugs. The cocaine was mentioned separately. I don't know if it is a separate item."

"They didn't mention drugs to me. Just booze."

"They told you she died of booze?"

He peered at the end of the cigarette he had just lit. "That doesn't make a lot of sense. The point was that she had died while drunk. An accident in the bathroom." His eyes lifted and met Kim's. "You're easy to talk to, do you know that? Now, don't tell me it's because you're a nun. You're no more a nun than that waitress." He nodded at the girl who had brought their drinks, an extremely well-endowed young lady whose skirt would have been short on a ballerina. "I mean, you weren't born a nun. You were born a woman."

"Actually, I was born a girl."

He waved the remark away as an irrelevancy. The plea in his eyes sought and found resonance in Kim. He had seemed such an improbable Lothario before, but she could sense now the attraction he had had for women: his helplessness. It was easy to want to mother this sad, glib Pagliaccio who elicited pity the more surely by denying he had any right to it.

"How old were you when you entered the convent?"

"My parents left me on the doorstep in a basket."

"Meaning you have known what is called the real world. Did you ever have a date?"

"Only Fig Newtons."

"I hate psychiatry, but there is a name for that kind of defense."

"And for your offensiveness too, I'm sure. We are here because you wanted to tell me your story. My biography wasn't part of the bargain."

"I'll bet it's harder because it is isn't hard anymore."

"What do you mean?"

"When you joined you must have expected to be locked away somewhere, the world well lost. And here you are, sitting in a bar with an old drunk, the girl you might have been if you had never taken the veil. I suppose the veil is only a metaphor now."

He might be drunk but he certainly was perceptive. How

many people understood, as he seemed to, the lure of self-abnegation?

Kim would not have entered into a discussion of it with Norman Shire sober, certainly not in his present condition, but there *was* a slight resentment that she was allowed to dress as she liked, to do as she liked, and to go on calling herself a nun. During the great debate that had riven the Order of Martha and Mary she had been only a novice, but she sided with those who spoke of playing a more decisive role in the world. It appealed to her idealism, to her American sense, that if something was wrong it ought to be righted. To live withdrawn from the world can be an indulgence, a luxury. A life of prayer. There was an unbaptized streak in Kim that did not really believe in the efficacy of prayer. If something was going to be done, she had to do it. But she had not joined the Order to change the world in that direct way, through social action. Her conception of the religious life was based on Sister Mary Teresa. It was the old nun's life she had wanted to emulate. Emtee Dempsey had been on the losing side in the great debate. Now the dust had settled, the winners had left, and she and Joyce and Emtee Dempsey lived alone in the house on Walton Street, their lives supported by an endowment preserved from the feverish handouts that had followed the sale of the college and property west of Chicago. There were times when Kim longed for the solitude and withdrawal a religious vocation had promised her. If she were to give up the ambitions and joys of the world, she should be free to abandon it. Now she pursued her doctorate and faced the prospect of a life indistinguishable from that of any other bachelor girl. As Emtee Dempsey would say, it was difficult to think this was the sort of *aggiornamento* Pope John XXIII had in mind. A thought had hovered on the edge of her mind during the funeral Mass and later at the cemetery. It could not be many years off that Sister Mary Teresa would die.

Nuns lived notoriously long lives, but even ten or fifteen more years left the bulk of Kim's life to be lived without the support of any vestige of the community of religious women founded by Blessed Abigail Keineswegs. There would be only Joyce and herself.

"We must pray," Emtee Dempsey said, whenever the future of the Order came up. "Among the possibilities are that the Order Blessed Abigail founded has served its purpose and is meant to fade away. It accomplished much in its day. Many holy women were among its members. Perhaps we were meant to be a casualty of all this post-conciliar nonsense. The periods after ecumenical councils have always been turbulent."

And off she went on an impromptu lecture, leaving Kim and Joyce to thoughts they found too frightening to discuss between themselves. Joyce sometimes said that she prayed for vocations every day. But what could it possibly mean to a young girl to join the Order of Martha and Mary in its present state of collapse? It was all well and good for Sister Mary Teresa to be philosophical about the fate of the Order. She would end her religious life as she had begun it, to the degree this was possible on Walton Street. The longer future Joyce and Kim faced was less comforting. How shrewd of Norman Shire to have guessed this.

"You're not drinking your juice," he said accusingly.

"I've drunk far more than I wanted already."

"Moderation," he mused. "That has always eluded me. If I drink at all, it must be to excess."

Like the larger crowd earlier, he had been moved from despondency by a few drinks.

Kim said, "You mustn't use Vivian Hoy's death as an excuse to kill yourself."

"Mustn't I? Where do all these rules and precepts come from anyway? What if we can do anything we damned please?"

"Well, I can't." Kim glanced at her watch. It had been forty-five minutes since they came down to the bar. "I'll have to check on Sister Mary Teresa."

"Is that your job, baby-sitting her?"

"Certainly not."

"What do you call it?"

"We are sisters in the same community. And I am her research assistant."

"Deputized to pay calls on Vivian and me. Why?"

What an annoying man he was. His tongue was loosened now and he really seemed to believe he was entitled to say anything that came into his head. It annoyed Kim to have her relation to Sister Mary Teresa put in terms she herself thought of when she was peeved at the old nun. All this frankness and insight could be tiresome.

She said, "Another little rule is that life doesn't amount to much if we don't have someone to look after."

Turnabout was obviously not fair play so far as Norman Shire was concerned. He looked at Kim as if she had just run a sword through his middle. "Thanks. I needed that."

"I really have to go."

"So go. And give my regards to Eugene Evans."

Kim had started to slide out of the booth but now she stopped. "You fellow owners don't seem to have much to say to one another."

"I only have twenty percent. I'm the poor relation. I preferred to let the Torrances and the Evanses squabble among themselves. Would you like to buy twenty percent of a women's soccer team?"

"What did they squabble about?"

"Ask them. Ask Diana. Better get upstairs to your ward."

"She is not my ward."

"Tell the waiter to stop by, will you?"

On her way out of the bar, Kim told the waiter to bring a large orange juice to the man with whom she had been sharing a booth.

Six

Although Diana returned to the house on Walton Street after the funeral, prompting Joyce to wonder if their prayers for vocations were finally being answered, Sister Mary Teresa did not question their guest about the quarreling Norman Shire had alleged went on between the Torrances and the Evanses.

"I think we should let a little time elapse. I don't want to prompt her into further lying."

"Has she admitted lying to you?"

"Not everything she said was lies."

"How long will she be staying with us?"

"Will there be other claims on the guest room?"

"Not that I know of."

"Good. I assured Diana she was welcome to stay as long as she liked."

A woman with an apartment in Chicago, a summer home in Wisconsin, and a thirty-foot boat anchored in Belmont Harbor did not seem in need of asylum. If anyone had a complaint about Diana's prolonged stay, it was Joyce. Their guest made no effort at all to help out, so Joyce had one more mouth to feed, one more person to look after. Of course Joyce was unlikely to complain. Kim did not like the thought that she alone resented Diana's presence among them. What on earth did Diana do all day?

"Oh, we talk about the Brass," Joyce said. "And we watch the soaps."

"You watch the soaps!"

"Emtee Dempsey told me to do everything to make her feel at home. She doesn't like to watch television alone. Those programs are incredible. But we can go on talking sports without losing the story line."

Joyce's obviously sincere interest in the Brass prompted Diana to call the team office and have her secretary bring over some team materials. Kim answered the door, and there on the porch stood Eileen West. They stared at each other for half a minute as mutual recognition slowly took place.

"What on earth are you doing here?" Eileen cried. Her hair seemed blonder than it had been in school and she wore it very short, a perfect style for her well-shaped head.

"I live here."

Eileen took a step backward and looked up in search of an address number. "Is Diana Torrance staying here?"

Eileen was the secretary Diana had phoned. Kim asked her in and the two women spoke their names, apparently unnecessarily. Kim took the package Eileen was carrying and they went down the hall to the parlor, where Joyce and Diana were watching television. Eileen wore a peppermint-striped suit and heels that seemed inches high. There was a brief hubbub in the parlor, but soon they left Diana unwrapping the package and went into the living room where they spent a moment marveling at how little and how much change the years had wrought.

"When did you leave, Kim?"

"Leave?"

"You did become a nun, didn't you?"

"Yes. But I haven't left. There are three of us here. . ."

"The little one who was at the funeral?"

"That's Sister Mary Teresa."

"She taught history, right?"

Kim found it hard to believe that anyone's memories of Emtee Dempsey could be vague. "We moved here after we sold the college."

"Who would want to buy a college?"

"You'd be surprised."

"Of course I never really cared for that place."

This, coupled with the question about Emtee Dempsey, shocked Kim. The college where she had been a student and where Sister Mary Teresa had been professor of medieval history was a mythical place for Kim. Revering it was like revering the womb that bore her. One of the cruelest blows of her life had been the realization that she was an alumna of a college that had ceased to be. Those who loved the college had always been critical of it, the expression of affectionate disappointment, but to say you hated the it! Of course, Kim's memories of Eileen West were vague. Vague yet faintly disturbing. There had been something odd about the way Eileen had left the campus.

"I didn't like the place and I was glad to leave it. What I really wanted was to see the world, so for most of a year I backpacked around Europe, half starving to death, but loving it. When I came back I got a job in a travel bureau. The promise was I would get to go all sorts of places at cut rates. Ha. Mainly that meant seats on Miami or New Orleans planes leaving at one in the morning were mine for the asking. But tell me about yourself. No, don't. Let's have lunch. But first I need a few minutes with Mrs. Torrance."

Emtee Dempsey, done with her stint for the day, was adding the new pages to the manuscript on her desk. It now stood some eight inches high. The old nun referred to that pile of pages as the Tower of Babel, but there was little doubt of the pride she felt in the book she was writing. And the sadness — in less than half a year the first draft would be complete. If she kept to her schedule, which was like assuming the sun would rise in the morning. She remembered Eileen West.

"Don't you?" she asked Kim.

"Oh, yes. I knew her at once. But I was never close to her."

"And now she works for the Chicago Brass?"

"As Diana's secretary."

Emtee Dempsey's frown could not have been described as a scowl. Kim explained the nature of the visit, adding that she and Eileen were having lunch together.

"Would you like to see her, Sister?"

"Not this morning," Emtee Dempsey said, and her pudgy little hands patted the pile of pages. Perhaps she was still preoccupied with her morning's work.

After quiche and salad and white wine, Kim and Eileen went on to the offices of the Chicago Brass so Kim could see where Eileen worked. "The scene of the crime," she called it at first, then regretted the phrase. An uncertain expression did not quite settle on her face.

"God knows what the future holds now, Kim. Phil Torrance, then Vivian Hoy. That girl was the franchise. We have played twice without her and lost both times. Now we're asking for a week of postponements, out of respect. Maybe we can make some quick trades and not lose too much ground."

Eileen's office was in a corner of the building: two walls of glass and two covered with photographs of Brass players — singly, in groups, as a team, in action, and posed.

"Phil had done a remarkable job building up the team, but Diana was a lot more help than he cared to admit."

"Are you in charge now?"

Eileen laughed. "It's almost that bad. No. Basically I am Publicity. There are seven, no eight, of us in the office, but without the Torrances, well. . ."

"I met Mr. Evans at the funeral."

"Now, there is an unmitigated pain in the you-know-what. If anyone was going to end up floating in the lake, I would have picked Evans. Both of them, him and Priscilla. For the right fee, I would have done it myself. After all, this is Chicago."

The description Eileen gave of relations between Evans and Torrance matched what Norman Shire had told her. She asked, "What did the two of them quarrel about?"

"The books. Accounting. Vivian Hoy. Evans wanted to sell her. Get top dollar while she's at the top of her form. Can you believe it? And the gate. He wanted figures after every game. His working assumption is that everyone cheats, so you can guess what his own practices must be."

Eileen smoked super-long double-filtered menthol cigarettes. At least she lit them. That entailed taking a puff, but from then on the cigarette seemed to function only as a smoking pointer to accent her remarks. It was like talking to a skywriter.

"Does Evans have an office here?"

"Of course. How else could he feel like a big shot? And when he isn't here, she is, Prissie, entertaining her society friends — a species of slumming, I suppose."

"Norman Shire has an office too?"

"Norman." Eileen made a face. "Do you know him?"

"I've met him."

"I don't suppose he'd try anything with a nun. No, I take that back. He was like Phil Torrance. It isn't even flattering when a man like that makes a pass at you. Anything with a skirt on."

"Was it true about Vivian Hoy and Mr. Torrance?"

"I suppose Diana told you."

"Well, she told Sister Mary Teresa. I gather it was true."

"You must be getting a terrible impression of the Brass. The place sounds like a zoo. I guess it is a zoo." Eileen lit another cigarette and silvery smoke curled upward through the sunlight. Between Norman Shire and Eileen, Kim had had the equivalent of a pack of cigarettes these past few days. Eileen regarded Kim through the shifting smoke. "I don't exempt myself either, Kim. I'm no angel."

"No one is."

"You are. I can tell. You're just what you were at school."

"I'm not sure I even wish that was true. In any case, it's not. If both Norman and Mr. Torrance were such animals, why do you dislike Mr. Evans so much more?"

"More? I don't dislike Norman or Mr. Torrance. They both understand sports. You would not believe the conversations those two could have about games played years ago, professional, college, it didn't matter, they could remember details. At first I thought it was a routine they had worked out. I mean, if they said Joe Blow hit into a double play in the third inning of the fourth game of the 1933 World Series, who could deny it? But I took notes and did some research and they were ninety-nine percent accurate. Eugene Evans couldn't tell you if there had been a World Series in 1933. Oh, he might know what the take was, but not what teams played in it, who won, or what the scores were. A funny thing. He was the only owner Vivian Hoy really respected."

"Oh?"

"No, it wasn't funny. She was a bit of a calculating machine herself. She was far and away the best one on the team, but soccer was a means to an end for her. She was probably as smart a woman as you'll ever meet. She had two dreams — to make a million and to go back to school. She and Evans could communicate. She wasn't even angry when he talked of selling her. All she said was, 'Better talk to Nelson first.'"

"Nelson?"

"Her agent. A lawyer. He has represented her ever since she joined the Brass. Of course Evans knew all about Nelson. It was Nelson who was smart enough to get her contract renegotiated every time it became clear that without Vivian there simply was no competitive team. Diana and Nelson always saved the day; Diana could deal with Nelson. From a purely business point of view, it made sense to sell her. Vivian understood that. Not that she proposed to be treated like a sack of flour."

Kim shook her head. "I really don't understand the least thing about contracts in professional sports. Can a player literally be sold? That makes them sound like slaves."

"Very well paid and generally happy slaves, but slaves."

"Eileen, why would Mrs. Torrance want us to think she had killed her husband?"

Although her cigarette was half burned, Eileen took a drag on it. She wore three rings on each hand and assorted necklaces from which dangled glittering objects of various kinds. "Did she actually say she had?"

"No. But she told us such a silly story, she practically invited us to become suspicious of her."

"She owns most of the Brass now," Eileen said musingly. "Not that she seems all that interested in it for the moment."

"She called and asked you to come to Walton Street."

"Sure. To bring some promotional stuff to show a fan."

"Eileen, did you know Vivian Hoy was on drugs?

"I'll never believe that's true. She did smoke. I knew her

secret there. I guess she figured I'd understand." Eileen made a little face. "But liquor and drugs? Not Vivian Hoy."

"That is how she died, Eileen. The medical report didn't leave much doubt of it."

A moment's pause, then Eileen gave out a little laugh. "Get a load of me, Miss Know-It-All. For all I know, the mayor sniffs cocaine. Maybe Phil's death was accidental too. He loved that boat, but he was about as much of a sailor as I am. Whenever he took it out he got seasick and he had trouble keeping his balance when it was riding at anchor. The boat was just a floating hideaway for him."

"Then you've been on it?"

"Sure. He liked to give parties out there. Don't get me wrong. Party parties. Half a dozen people, as many as ten. Boats are fun, safe at anchor like that."

"Is it possible that he just fell and bumped his head and went on into the water?"

"How would I know? He had a habit of falling off the boat, I can tell you that. At parties, he did it deliberately. 'Making a big splash,' he called it. Oh, he was the life of the party, Phil."

"That was generally known, that he fell into the water as a joke?"

She looked at Kim. "Of course."

"Who would go to his parties, Eileen?"

"What on earth would you want to know for?"

Kim smiled. "Let me tell you about Sister Mary Teresa, Eileen."

Philip Torrance was interred in Chicago; Vivian Hoy's body was shipped back to Davenport, Iowa, for burial. Contrary to predictions—Eileen West's, Norman Shire's, the bulk of the sports world—the Chicago Brass, after a week of postponements, enjoyed a winning streak. Players who had been overshadowed by Vivian Hoy suddenly came alive and, as if a throne were vacant and they candidates for it, began to play with verve and daring. The fans responded. At first they came out much as many had come to Philip Torrance's wake, out of sympathy and respect, but the winning streak caught the imagination of the town, and women's soccer news got more than its fair share of space on the sports pages of the city papers.

"For the first time they're playing as a team," Joyce observed.

"Either we play together or we get put out to pasture together," Millie Provost, the coach, said. A wiry little woman, she shifted her weight from foot to foot and kept her eye on the camera rather than the interviewer. "We can make the playoffs. Nobody can ask for more than that."

Several players said with varying degrees of articulateness that they intended to give it their best shot, think of it as winning one for Vivian if you want to. (This suggestion came from a cigar-chewing writer who usually covered the Notre Dame teams. Like most American commentators, having learned the rudiments of soccer, he had changes to suggest that would turn it into a genuine sport.) Sister Mary Teresa, hands joined over the head of her cane, seated on the edge of her chair, frowned at the television.

"Millie Provost is on the list Eileen West gave you, isn't she?"

"Yes. But none of the players."

There were nineteen names on the list Eileen tapped out on her typewriter for Kim. There had been eighteen until Kim reminded Eileen of herself. "Right," Eileen had said, and rolled the paper back into the machine. Rat-a-tat-tat, and she was done. Kim had been somewhat deflated by Sister Mary Teresa's reaction to the list. She scarcely glanced at it, letting it flutter to her desk as her eyes drifted over Kim's head. Kim waited, but the old nun seemed merely distracted.

"Is something wrong, Sister?"

The clear blue eyes regarded Kim for a moment through

rimless lenses. "Sit down, Sister. How much do you know of the Eileen West matter?"

The Eileen West matter? Kim sat. "Tell me."

"It is not a pretty story, but it is an old story and one I had all but forgotten. Perhaps we do remember the good things best. Something to think about there. I mean from the point of view of historical methodology. The received opinion is that it is the bad things that get recorded and the good forgot. Certainly news is usually bad news. The cliché that history is the victor's version may not carry the weight it is thought to carry." Her eyes narrowed and she pulled her lower lip between her teeth.

"Eileen West," Kim reminded her.

In school Eileen had stolen a test and planted it in another girl's room. It might have been done without malice, merely out of panic at the thought of being discovered with the exam; but then, she could have destroyed it. Eileen had wanted to get the other girl into trouble and she had very nearly succeeded. A room search had been authorized when it was discovered that the test was missing (the professor numbered copies of his test lightly in pencil on the reverse side and knew at a glance a copy was missing and the number it bore). The girl in whose room the test was found was the last person who needed to cheat in order to pass. The intended victim was not only intelligent, she was also shrewd. Asked to explain why anyone would want to discredit her, she mentioned her rival with a young man. The rival was Eileen West. Confronted with the charge and offhand remarks about fingerprints, Eileen crumbled and confessed. Her attempt to discredit her rival ended her own college career.

Her shame had not been publicized, but rumors swept the campus and everyone knew something awful explained Eileen's dismissal. It was good to see how far she had come despite that youthful indiscretion, Kim thought.

"Yes," Emtee Dempsey said.

*　　*　　*

One afternoon the doorbell rang and a short bald man with an open shirt and an enormous belly announced that he was Mr. Nelson and would appreciate having a word with the renowned Sister Mary Teresa. Joyce, who had answered the door, put him in the living room and went to the study to repeat verbatim what the caller had said. Emtee Dempsey's brows rose above her own spectacles. "Bring him to me and then go upstairs and tell Sister Kimberly to join us."

"I won't be able to myself. I'm baking."

Joyce seldom succeeded in getting a rise out of the old nun. "Very well. We are all counting on you for a very special meal tonight."

Kim came downstairs reluctantly, her head chock-full of thoughts of Charles the Bald, on whom she was writing a paper. Nelson was seated across the desk from Sister Mary Teresa, holding a large cigar in a pudgy hand adorned with a diamond pinkie ring. He had been told they would be joined by Kim, so there was only the slightest interruption before he got back to what he was saying. It seemed to be an extended eulogy of Sister Mary Teresa, on whose exploits Nelson was thoroughly informed.

"The entry in *Who's Who* is modest to a fault, Sister."

"Is it? Then you must blame Sister Kimberly. She sends in the update each year."

Nelson gave Kim a forgiving smile. "I suppose *Who's Who* is not the best vehicle for the full story. In any case, Sister, you see sitting before you one of your most intense admirers. As an admirer I could scarcely be indifferent to the fact that your young colleague here called on my client shortly before her death."

"Vivian Hoy?"

"That is right. Given your past, I can only assume you have some insight into the reason for her death."

"That scarcely takes insight, Mr. Nelson. The police have made it a public matter that she died of a fatal mixture and/or overdose of liquor and drugs."

"A judgment you don't for a minute believe."

"I will take that to be an elliptical expression of your own skepticism about the verdict."

"Vivian Hoy did not drink, Sister. As for drugs, it is ludicrous to imagine she would deliberately harm her body. Her body, her athletic prowess, was her fortune."

"One reads every day of athletes who take drugs, Mr. Nelson. They have every bit as much incentive to avoid them as did Vivian Hoy."

"It is not a theoretical matter with me. I know she neither drank nor took drugs."

"Meaning that she was not in the habit of doing either. All the more reason, perhaps, why a single indiscretion proved fatal."

Nelson shook his head. From the inside pocket of his sports coat he drew forth a small notebook. He slapped it against his other hand several times and then tossed it on the desk. "That is Vivian's diary. I guess you can call it a diary. It will strengthen your suspicion that her death was not accidental."

"How did you come into possession of that?" Emtee Dempsey's hands gripped the arms of her chair but her gaze was riveted on the little notebook.

"I took it from her apartment."

"The police overlooked it?"

Nelson chewed on his cigar and looked back and forth from Emtee Dempsey to Kim almost furtively. "I'm going to say something in confidence. Which is nonsense. How can I confide in two people? I am going to trust you with my life. I went to Vivian's apartment hours before the Brass got worried and sent someone over. I found her dead. There's no point in trying to describe my feelings. Sure, the girl was a gold mine, but I liked her. She had great athletic skill, but she had a mind too." He nodded at the notebook. "You'll see. I found her dead and I didn't report it. I'm a lawyer, I know what that makes me. But I just couldn't pick up the phone and make the call. I don't know. In part I had the crazy notion that so long as no one knew, it hadn't really happened."

"You found her in bed. How did she look?"

"She wasn't in bed. She was slumped over the table."

"She was!"

Nelson looked to Kim for help and, finding none, asked Sister Mary Teresa the reason for her surprise.

"Mr. Nelson, are you being perfectly frank with me?"

"Am I being frank with you? I tell you I discovered the body and didn't report it, and you want to know if I am leveling?"

"Don't you realize that according to the police report she was discovered dead in her bed?"

"She was in pajamas..."

"No. It was quite specific. The body was found in the bed. Sister Kimberly, who was it from the Brass who went to the apartment to check on Vivian Hoy and found her dead?"

"Eileen West."

Why did she feel like a snitch in saying that? Now they had both Vivian Hoy's dossier from the offices of the Chicago Brass and what Nelson called her diary. Kim was trying to remember if the newspaper reports had been as explicit about the body's being found in bed as Emtee Dempsey was insisting.

"I don't understand," Nelson said.

"Neither do I. That is a species of wisdom, knowing that one does not understand. There are several possibilities. One, you are lying. We eliminate that."

"Thank you."

"At least temporarily. Second, a third person was at the apartment, arriving after you left and leaving before Eileen West arrived. Or, third, Eileen West moved the body from the table to the bed before sounding the alarm."

"Why should she do that?"

"It could be entirely trivial. She might have thought it

would be more decorous if the body were found laid out in state rather than crumpled at the table."

"I thought she had fallen asleep there. Her head was resting on her arm, her eyes closed. But when I touched her, she was cold and rigid." Nelson shivered and sought solace in his cigar.

"On the other hand, it could be very significant indeed. I shall proceed on the assumption that it is. If the body was showing signs of rigor, it would be no easy matter to move it from the table to the bed. And it would be necessary to dispose the limbs . . ." Emtee Dempsey stopped. Kim had let out a sound of horrified protest. "Very well, Sister. We will respect your sensibilities. No matter. Someone moved the dead body of Vivian Hoy and that is the first ray of light we have received."

"Light? But what does it illumine?"

"It will tell us who murdered Vivian Hoy and Philip Torrance."

Nelson blinked. "And I thought I was bringing you only that diary."

Emtee Dempsey steepled her fingers and squinted through her spectacles. "Tell me all about Mr. Evans."

"All about him? You don't have that much time."

"We have all the time in the world, don't we, Sister Kimberly?"

Although she simply nodded, Kim imagined the face Joyce would make in the circumstances, and nodding came easier. She did not find Nelson's account of the Evanses very illuminating, but sitting through it seemed a small price to pay in order to see Vivian Hoy's diary.

Evans, in Nelson's account, was a thorn in his side, forever pressing to sell Vivian Hoy's contract to another team for huge sums of money.

"Wouldn't that have been to her advantage?"

"Vivian wouldn't have seen a nickel of it."

"Nor you?"

"What do you know about the arrangement between an agent and an athlete, Sister?"

"Explain it to me."

"It's simple as sin. Unless my client gets something, I get nothing. My cut is ten percent and ten percent of nothing..."

"Is nothing. If she is worth so much on the open market, why can't she demand more from the Chicago Brass?"

"Exactly! I do the demanding, of course. But you have hit upon my argument. I have been renegotiating her contract on just the basis you suggest."

"And Mr. Evans doesn't like it?"

"Think of it. It's money out of his pocket. He has the soul of a banker. I wish he'd fallen off *his* boat. Not that the others like it any better. I thought Phil Torrance would choke me to death when I brought it up. Shire? You would have thought I'd insulted Pele. Of course they thought Evans was crazy to even think of selling Vivian. Diana I could reason with. She knew Vivian's worth. The girl was the team, it was as simple as that."

"Mr. Evans was very useful to you."

"You're kidding."

"His desire to sell was the basis of your negotiating."

"That wasn't his intention. Eugene Evans is interested in Eugene Evans, period."

"And now Vivian Hoy is dead."

"Yeah." Nelson looked suddenly abject. "And I don't have to tell you what ten percent of a dead client amounts to."

It seemed to sum the man up. Obviously he had regarded Vivian Hoy as a commodity, ten percent of which belonged to him. This robbed his criticism of Evans of any moral force. If he could have received ten percent of the sale, no doubt he would have been egging Evans on. He had played with a cigar for minutes before taking Emtee Dempsey at her word and lighting it. He sat there, seemingly enclosed in the easy chair across the desk from the old nun, wizened and shrewd and somehow Oriental with all the smoke surrounding him. Kim had never before appreciated the notion of a smoke screen. She found herself fascinated by the shapes and hues of the smoke as it swirled around Nelson, rising up into the lampshade beside the chair as if thereby fulfilling its destiny. It was fascinating, almost, making it possible to ignore the pungent odor of the cigar. How Emtee Dempsey, for whom cigarette smoke was torture, could tolerate Nelson's cigar, Kim did not understand. It wasn't as if she was learning anything of importance from the babble of the agent.

"Do you take a drink, Mr. Nelson?"

"Nobody's perfect, Sister."

"I am not reprimanding you. I am offering you something. Would you like some whiskey?"

"You have some here?" Nelson leaned forward, emerging from a cloud, and looked at Emtee Dempsey with a devilish little smile.

"We have a drop or two of Irish whiskey left, I think. A gift of a student. Would you serve Mr. Nelson, Sister?"

Kim got up. "Can I bring you something, Sister Mary Teresa?"

Not to be outdone, Emtee Dempsey drew a watch from her pocket and frowned at it for a moment. "I don't think so. Too early."

Kim did not close the study door when she left the room. Some ventilation would help.

"The Jameson's?" Joyce said. "That's been gone for months. Your brother Richard had the last of it."

"Do we have any whiskey at all?"

"There's some bourbon Katherine left. A Christmas gift she didn't want."

"Let him drink that then."

"Want a taste?"

"No!"

"I just asked." Joyce poured a little dollop for herself into a water glass and tossed it off. Her eyes widened and she began to blink furiously. "Awful," she groaned when she caught her breath.

"Good," Kim said enigmatically and started back in the direction of the cigar smoke.

It was fun to listen to Nelson go on about the bouquet of the Irish whiskey he was drinking, prodded by Emtee Dempsey, who sounded as if she were working on commission for Jameson's.

Finally Nelson finished his whiskey. He took his cue from Emtee Dempsey, who rose from her chair when Nelson at last put the empty glass on the table beside him. Perhaps it was because he was so short himself that he realized Emtee Dempsey was on her feet. There were those who failed to notice the difference between Emtee Dempsey seated and Emtee Dempsey standing.

The old nun went down the hall to the door with Nelson, a courtesy Kim had not imagined she would extend to the agent. They even spent some minutes talking at the door. Meanwhile Kim opened the study window and took Nelson's ashtray to the kitchen. Emtee Dempsey was behind her desk once more when Kim returned to the study.

"You are the soul of charity, Sister," Kim said.

"I am not. Uncharitableness is my major weakness."

"Well, you were certainly kind to Mr. Nelson."

"The man is a gold mine." Emtee Dempsey rocked back in her chair, a pleased smile on her face. "Even his cigar smelled pleasant." The old nun seemed perfectly serious.

"You mean he would like to represent a gold mine."

"You are being cynical. No, naive. Do you think it culpable for a man to engage in business? I am sure he performs a useful service for his clients. Did you follow what he said?"

"I listened."

"He himself did not realize the significance of the remark."

"What remark?"

"Come, come. You're teasing."

Kim tipped her head to one side, narrowed her eyes, and made a thin line of her lips. If either of them was teasing, it was Sister Mary Teresa. "Did you believe what he said about finding the body?"

"You are skeptical because you dislike the man. And that can be an impediment when one is seeking a murderer."

"You think Nelson is a murderer?"

The question momentarily surprised the old nun. "He could be, of course. Anyone could be. I was referring to his offhand remark about the Evans boat."

"What about it?"

"Sister Kimberly, perhaps I do you an injustice. That was certainly the first inkling I had that Evans too has a boat anchored in Belmont Harbor."

"He didn't say that."

"Ah, you were listening. I will wager the boat is kept where Philip Torrance kept his. You must find out if I am right."

"I'll stop by the harbor in the morning."

"Surely there is an easier way to find out. Aren't boats registered or something? Telephone the harbor and ask."

The Evanses' boat was anchored in Belmont Harbor. Emtee Dempsey smiled as if some breakthrough hypothesis had just survived a crucial test.

"What does it mean?" Kim asked.

"Ah," Emtee Dempsey said, her smile fading. "That is the next question." And, gripping the arms of her chair, the little nun stared straight ahead, but Kim knew her eyes were not recording what was there in the study. Kim said good night, but she might just as well have addressed the desk as the person behind it.

Seven

Whether or not Emtee Dempsey had read the diary of Vivian Hoy remained a matter of conjecture as noon of the following day approached. Kim might have asked, but she was too stubborn to put the question to the old nun. So she suffered through a discussion of the typescript of the most recent chapter of Sister Mary Teresa's massive history of the twelfth century; and when they were done and Emtee Dempsey picked up her fountain pen and went back to work composing, Kim stormed out of the study.

"Ask her, for heaven's sake," Joyce said. "You're getting as pigheaded as she is."

"I should not have to ask her. She knows I want to see it."

"Maybe she hasn't read it herself yet."

"Ha!"

"I'd like to see that diary myself."

"Why don't you ask her for it?"

"Okay." Joyce put down her coffee mug and marched out of the kitchen. Kim strained to hear, even though she expected an easily audible explosion. The old nun did not like frivolous interruptions while in the throes of composition. She heard Joyce's sharp rap on the study door, heard the door open and in mere seconds close again. And then there was the sound of Joyce returning. She sailed into the kitchen holding aloft the notebook with a florid cover that Nelson had given Emtee Dempsey the night before.

"All you have to do is ask," Joyce said. "She said she realized Vivian was one of my heroines so my curiosity is understandable."

"Let me see it."

"Pretty please."

"Joyce!" She could not make her voice menacing. She felt like a fool. Joyce was right. She was becoming as childish as Emtee Dempsey. Joyce gave her the notebook.

They read it together at the kitchen table, sipping coffee, not saying a word. There was something eerie about reading the large girlish scrawl of Vivian Hoy, realizing that she was dead. And something illicit, too. It was like reading someone else's mail. And a diary is even more personal than mail. At least it should be. Vivian Hoy's was not. She had the habit of giving her own accounts of games, emphasizing the goals she had scored. Maybe the entries could be dated by ascertaining when those games had been played. It was surprising that someone so eager to write of those contests had not noted their dates. When she wrote about other things, it was difficult to follow, since she used so many initials and abbreviations. It was Joyce who came up with an important interpretation. There were increasing references to PT-109.

"That was John Kennedy's boat," Kim said.

"Boat. Of course. PT means Philip Torrance."

Joyce was right. Vivian must have been inspired by her first sail on the Torrance boat. That voyage could now be made out from an entry referring to B.H. and B.C. Belmont Harbor and the *Brass Cupcake*, the name of the Torrance boat. But apart from the pet name for Phil Torrance, the abbreviating seemed due to Vivian's hurry rather than to secretiveness. It was not so much a code as a species of shorthand. They came to the last page and sat staring at it. Kim felt a wave of sadness wash over her. Vivian could have had no idea that the game in St. Louis would be her last or that she was writing her last entry. Kim returned the diary to the study. Sister Mary Teresa took it without a word and put it back in her drawer.

"Thank you," Kim said, hoping to goad some comment from Emtee Dempsey.

Tiny blue eyes looked up at her. "Sister Kimberly, I would like you to go to Belmont Harbor after all."

It was a lowering day and far out the gray of the lake blended into the gray of the sky without benefit of horizon. The protected basin of Belmont Harbor looked calm by comparison with the open lake, but even there the anchored boats swung on their anchors and bobbed rhythmically, their masts the measure of their movement. A few adventurers were sailing within the protection of the causeway — small boats, even a sunfish or two, their single sails billowing and then collapsing in the unpredictable wind.

Kim had been told that Jason Smally was out there in his Laser. She would not have known a Laser from a three-masted schooner if she had not been told it was a single-sail craft. Some surly kids, two boys and a girl lounging by the boathouse, had told her that Jason was sailing. Small-craft warnings apparently did not apply to such intraharbor sailing. She walked away from her informants, wishing she had worn slacks. The wind whipped at her skirt and she felt a little silly holding it down. It seemed to make her more vulnerable to the lounging insolent curiosity of those kids by the boathouse. They wore the spoiled look of the affluent, and the boy she had addressed had honey-colored hair and a knowledgeable look Kim found upsetting. The girl beside him, emerging ripely from her swimsuit, sun-bleached hair, a pagan look, was no better. Kim was able to forget her unease only when she got far enough away from the boys and was concentrating on a boat she thought might be Jason's.

The boat had been tacking into the wind as it made its way to the mouth of the harbor and now swung round, its sail belly-ing as it caught the wind, picking up speed. Kim had never seen a sailboat go so fast. The Laser was tipped and seemed to be running on its side, with the boy sailing it plainly visible. He seemed to be exulting in the skill it took to keep the boat moving at such a rate and at so dangerous an angle to the water. That angle seemed to Kim to narrow and then, in the wink of an eye, the boat went over, coming to an abrupt stop in the process. Kim cried out as she watched, and when the boat lay helplessly on its side in the water she looked wildly around to see if others had seen the accident. The boys by the boathouse were laugh-ing. They could not have noticed the danger Jason was in. Kim ran back to them.

"That boat tipped over! I think it's Jason Smally."

The girl looked at Kim with eyes that suggested she was not in complete touch with the real world. The boy stood and look-ed languidly out at the harbor. "Yeah, that's Jason."

"Aren't you going to do something?"

There was the sound of snickers. The blond's smile sent only one corner of his mouth up. "Don't worry about Jason. He spends half the day in the water."

Kim looked out to where the dumped sailor was now visible, his hands clutching the side of the overturned boat while he got his feet up onto the exposed centerboard. The boat came slowly upright and Jason scrambled over the side and began to gather in the lines. In a moment the Laser was proceeding sedately before the wind, heading for the dock.

When he came onto the dock, Jason Smally looked like a drowned puppy. His hair was wild and wet and his tee shirt was plastered to his body. Shivering, he looked at Kim with eyes that were bloodshot and ringed with spiky lashes.

"You're the one who found Philip Torrance's body, aren't you?"

He nodded. "You a reporter?"

"Aren't you cold?" His shivering seemed to increase.

"Let me get a towel."

Kim stayed where she was, looking down at the boat he had tied fore and aft. How little it looked. There was no way the boom could swing unless the sailor ducked, and though it was aluminum and probably light, Kim could imagine it would not be pleasant to be struck by it. The shallow cockpit was half full of water from the spill. Despite its present unprepossessing appearance, Kim felt a desire to sail the little boat. It was one of those desires doomed to remain a velleity. She had lived within easy access to this lake all her life and had never once been on it in a boat. Jason came back, toweling his head vigorously still wearing the wet tee shirt. The girl was with him.

"This is Wilma."

Shaking hands would have been inappropriate. Kim nodded and the girl's gray eyes slid past her.

"Which boat belongs to the Evanses?" she asked.

He considered a moment, then pointed. "Forty footer. That's pretty big. It's a shame he doesn't use it more often. I mean for sailing."

"How much is often?"

"More than never. I can count the times I've seen that boat

go out. Of course he needs a good-size crew, but that's no problem around here. Evans needs more than crew. He's only a passenger on his own boat. I suppose that's why he uses it mainly as a place to have parties."

"Have you been aboard her?"

"I sailed on it once," Wilma said. Her lower lip resumed its pout.

"I've been on it." A faraway look came into Jason's eye as he said this. "Why is it always people like that who can afford the good boats?"

Kim sensed resentment in these kids, as she had earlier at the boathouse. Did they loll about the harbor all day envying the men who had earned enough money to buy such craft, men who probably included their own fathers? Belmont Harbor did not seem a very good place to develop one's vision of life.

"Were the Evanses on their boat the day Philip Torrance drowned?"

"Yes."

"You seem very sure."

"I am. They slept aboard that night. They must have. They were getting into their car in the parking lot when I came. There were only two other cars besides mine. The Evanses were coming from their boat."

"How do you know?"

The bone in the bridge of his nose was visible beneath the skin and it gave him somehow an untamed look, almost that of an Indian, perhaps an illusion fostered by his weathered appearance and the clothing he wore. "They were. It just figures. No one shows up at that hour. Certainly not the Evanses. And they were dressed in boat clothes. I think they were a little drunk. I waved at them but no response, not that that's any big surprise. Kids are invisible to them."

"How much after you saw the Evanses did you find the body?"

"As soon as I went down to the dock."

"Were the Evanses still there?"

"No. The first thing I thought of was to tell them. But when I ran up to the parking lot, they were already pulling out."

"They might have found the body," Kim murmured.

"They should have. I suppose if they were hung over they just wanted to get out of here."

"I suppose."

"What paper do you write for?"

"I'm not a journalist," Kim said.

"You're not?"

"I'm a nun."

Wilma laughed, the sound rushing out, but then she stopped and looked at Kim as if she were trying to focus her eyes. She said, "I don't want to be in the paper again anyway."

Jason and Wilma walked with her toward the parking lot. As she had with Vivian Hoy, Kim felt like an imposter. Perhaps if she had not been feeling so guilty she would have figured out who Wilma was before she was halfway back to Walton street.

It was that afternoon that Diana Moore Torrance, in Joyce's phrase, came clean.

"I haven't been completely candid with you," she said, eyes cast down, her voice betraying anything but contrition.

"Oh?" Emtee Dempsey said, casting a glance at Kim and Joyce. There was a rustle as Katherine drew herself up as if to sit at attention in her chair. Or was it the posture of a judge about to pass sentence?

The time was five-thirty in the afternoon. Katherine had come by for a drink and had wisely decided against the Irish whiskey Emtee Dempsey urged upon her. ("People do seem to like it so," the old nun said.) It was clear that Sister Mary Teresa had an intimation of what Diana wanted to say. Earlier in the afternoon their guest had come by the study to say she thought it best to terminate her stay in the house on Walton Street. She turned down the suggestion of a farewell banquet; this impromptu cocktail party was what Emtee Dempsey called a *pis aller.*

"I thought of just going away and saying nothing, but you have all been so kind to me, I can't."

"I hope you're not saying you lied to me?" Emtee Dempsey spoke in a small voice. Joyce's eyes rolled heavenward and Kim sighed. It was clear this was to be a time for high drama.

"I feel that I misled you."

Sister Mary Teresa occupied her chair as a thrown pillow might. An imaginary sword transfixed her where her heart should be. "If you are referring to your effort to make it look as if you had killed your husband, have no fear. I never believed it for a moment."

Katherine, having taken half her wine in a single swallow, put down the glass noisily. "Well I did. I believed it right up to the point when Vivian Hoy's body was found."

Katherine had a point. It was the death of Vivian Hoy that took Diana off the hook, since she could not have been guilty of that. But her visit prior to her husband's death and the way she had fled to Walton Street from Belmont Harbor that fateful morning seemed designed to draw suspicion on herself. Nor did she deny it now. If Emtee Dempsey took this with exaggerated equanimity, Katherine did not.

"Between you and Norman Shire your husband's death has become a ludicrous matter. People who could not possibly have been responsible rush forward to confess murder."

"Norman says he killed Philip?"

"Yes," Katherine said with heavy irony. "Apparently by long distance from Peoria."

"How far is it from Peoria?" Emtee Dempsey asked.

"Don't suggest that you give credence to Norman Shire's absurd claim."

"Diana, why don't you tell us what did happen that night?"

Diana's new story had the merit of jibing with facts that could be verified by others. She had driven to the airport to meet her husband and the team. Millie Provost and others would vouch for that.

"Phil suggested going to the boat and we did, and everything was pretty much as I told you. Except that, when I left the boat, Vivian Hoy came with me. Phil and Pearson remained behind, more than half drunk, with a girl who was half their age and apparently twice as drunk. I think Vivian saw for the first time how Phil made me feel."

"Vivian denied going to the boat."

"She was there."

"Are you trying to make Vivian Hoy look like your husband's killer?"

"No! I admit that I acted foolishly," Diana said sharply. The pose of penitent widow had been dropped.

"But you have neglected to say why," Emtee Dempsey said. "Why did you deliberately draw suspicion down on yourself?"

"I knew nothing could happen to me. After all, I hadn't done it."

"Whom were you protecting?"

"Protecting?"

"Your story had the effect, however briefly, of diverting the attention of the police. No doubt that was your motive."

"But that's silly. Why should I want to protect the one who killed Phil, even if I knew who he was?"

"And who went on to kill Vivian Hoy as well." Katherine had finished her sauterne and now flourished her glass at Joyce, who took it away for a refill. "Now that you have eliminated yourself, who do you think killed your husband?"

"I don't know."

"Surely you've thought about it."

"Sister, it could have been any of a dozen people."

"Name them."

"Phil was a ruthless man — in business, in life. He made a lot of enemies."

"He made a lot of friends as well, I gather," Katherine said sardonically.

"Women friends? Yes. I suppose some of his discards had a motive too."

"But none as great as your own," Emtee Dempsey said.

"Do you really think I did it? Sister, I was home weeping in bed when it happened. I was crying for myself, self-pity, but I suppose I was crying for Phil too, for what used to be. It was that damnable soccer team that ruined us. It was a huge success and it ruined us. I wish we had never heard of it."

Emtee Dempsey allowed a moment to pass. "Let us, as Katherine suggests, review our roster. Sister Kimberly has learned that the Evanses were on their boat in Belmont Harbor on the night your husband was killed."

Diana sat very still, looking at the old nun with widened eyes. Her whole body seemed to move when she turned slowly toward Kim. "Is that true?"

Kim nodded. Joyce came back with Katherine's drink and the reporter wanted to know what difference it made if the Evanses had been on their boat.

The significance that emerged haltingly from what Diana said, mainly in answer to questions, was that the enmity between the Evanses and Philip Torrance had reached a flash point the day prior to her husband's death. The subject was money. Evans had invested in the Brass in order to make money and he was enthused about a feeler they had received from a club in the east. The Brass would receive a million-dollar bonus if Vivian signed a two-year contract with the Jersey Jills for the same amount. It would have been the largest contract in the history of women's soccer. To accept the offer made sense in terms of quick money, but Philip Torrance was adamantly opposed. It would ruin the Brass. Evans said they could buy an entire team with the profits. Philip said if he thought that, he was dumber than he looked. Voices rose. Torrance offered to buy Evans out, but the deal could not be in cash and Evans rejected it disdainfully. He was already up to his ears in promises. What had Norman Shire made of such feuding?

"He stayed away. He refused to be the one to settle the matter, taking sides. Evans told him he was already doing that by refusing to explore the offer for Vivian. Of course Norman did not want Vivian leaving the Brass, and Chicago."

"Was Eugene Evans capable of violence?"

Sister Mary Teresa put the question to Eileen West when she came to pick up Diana after the former student and old teacher had made brief reference to the past. Eileen did not take off her sunglasses when she came into the house, declined the offer of a drink, but was willing enough to address the question put to her out of the blue.

"They were about the same size. Featherweights. Once Eugene Evans threw a paperweight at Mr. Torrance. He missed, but broke the glass case where Mr. Torrance kept his awards and plaques and things like that."

"Is that how that got broken?" Diana said.

"Then Philip got violent. Mrs. Evans and I had to pry them apart."

"Where was I?" Diana asked.

"It was the day you said you were going on retreat."

"The day I came here! That was the day I came to see you. Oh, Sister Mary Teresa, I've brought nothing but trouble to your house."

"Now, now. I'll walk you to the door." And, leaning on Diana and Eileen West, Emtee Dempsey left the room.

Katherine contemplated her second drink. "I needed this," she announced and took a healthy sip. "Am I the only one drinking? Can't you two at least have sherry, for heaven's sake. I feel like a lapsed alcoholic whenever I drink in this house."

"Kim could have some Irish whiskey," Joyce suggested.

"No, thanks."

"Pour Emtee Dempsey some sherry," Katherine urged. "She'll drink it if you do. Waste not, want not."

They heard the front door close and then the thump of Emtee Dempsey's cane as she returned down the hall. Joyce scooted back from the kitchen with the sherry just as the old nun was lowering herself into her chair.

"For me?"

"Katherine ordered it."

"And I was just going to ask for some of our legendary Irish whiskey. Ah well. Cheers."

"Your old student is a great disappointment, Sister," Katherine said when they were done toasting each other.

"Sister Kimberly?"

"I was thinking of Diana Torrance."

"You had hoped she was a murderer?"

"Ha. I do not agree that she endangered herself in order to protect someone. I changed my mind about that when Vivian Hoy was killed, because Diana was snug as a bug in this house at the time. Whether or not she could account for her whereabouts when her husband was killed, she was out. The two killings are connected."

Sister Mary Teresa said, "One knew she was not telling the truth."

Kim made a face. "Did one?"

Emtee Dempsey ignored her. "Think the worst of the woman, give her credit for truly diabolical cunning. Then her transparent lies become part of a larger scheme. Item, some days before the death of her husband she visits here and sets the scene. When the body of her husband is discovered floating in the lake, she flies to us for sanctuary. Her story would lead even the best-disposed to conjecture that Diana has done away with her husband. I take the bait, at least apparently, wondering what she is really trying to accomplish."

"You think she was protecting someone?"

"I considered it."

She sipped her sherry. If that sip were typical, it would take her three weeks to empty the glass.

"Because Diana was in this house when the foul deed was done," Katherine said.

"She might very well have been in her apartment, weeping in her bed, when her husband was killed and that would still not have deterred my suspicions. No, if she was intent on protecting someone, then it is that someone who is of interest to me."

"And who would that be?"

"There is a prior question."

"What is that?"

"Was she right to think that someone is in need of protection?"

"Are you suggesting that Diana, like her husband, had outside amorous interests?"

Sister Mary Teresa frowned and puckered her lips. "I would like to know whom the police suspect. They have their choice among the partners, Evans and Shire."

"They might kill him, but why Vivian? Norman Shire considered himself in love with her; Evans considered her an investment."

"And so did her agent, Nelson. No one had any reason to wish Vivian Hoy dead. Was she hated by the team?"

"Quite the contrary. They loved her more than the fans did."

Kim said, "Perhaps she did commit suicide. Maybe Philip Torrance's death was too much for her. Marriage to a wealthy man, once he had divorced Diana, went out the window."

"Or overboard," Katherine said. "No. Diana is the one with motives. Her wishes could have been carried out by someone who did not share her motives."

"And who might that be?"

For twenty minutes they pored over the list of boat guests Eileen West had provided Kim, but neither of the old women could find a name that filled the role they were imagining.

"We might just as well suspect Pearson," Katherine said disgustedly.

"Or Wilma," Kim said.

Two old pairs of eyes turned on her. "Wilma?"

"The girl who was with Pearson on his yacht and who visited the Torrance boat with him."

"Tush," Katherine said. "We wouldn't even know about her if she hadn't told the police. Speaking of whom, they reached a standstill days ago. I am told there is strong sentiment in the coroner's office to classify Vivian Hoy's death as self-inflicted. The death of Philip Torrance could then very well be called an accident."

"Whatever label is put on those deaths, they are murders, connected murders. There is no doubt of it. How dare the police sweep them under the rug?"

"It is not so simple, Sister. There is a financial crunch. Investigations cost money even when you know what you're looking for. The police have no suspects."

"No suspects! Sister Kimberly, is this true? What does Richard say?"

"To me? Not much at the moment."

"Call him."

"I'll dial the number."

"I suppose he is having his dinner now."

"Why don't we see if he's still in his office." Kim wanted to call the old nun's bluff. She also wanted to hear from Richard whether there were any leads on the Torrance and Hoy deaths. Just so Emtee Dempsey bore the onus of butting in where they didn't belong.

Richard was just leaving the office and he agreed reluctantly to stop by Walton Street on his way home when Emtee Dempsey told him she had important information on the Hoy and Torrance murders. She put down the phone wearing a tightlipped expression of satisfaction.

"What will you tell him?" Katherine asked. Although she was far from being a shrinking violet herself, Katherine never failed to be surprised by Emtee Dempsey's brazenness.

"I didn't say that I had anything to tell him he did not already know."

"I'm not sure I want to stay for this," Katherine said.

"You may miss an important story."

"Oh, for heaven's sake. Don't try to con me too."

Emtee Dempsey gave her old friend the fish eye. "Katherine, at this very moment I am ninety-five percent certain who murdered Phil Torrance and Vivian Hoy."

"Tush. You are bluffing shamelessly."

"Think what you like. But, as you do, ask yourself how often I have failed you in the past."

"All right, who's your candidate?"

Emtee Dempsey wagged a pudgy finger. "All in good time. But I have made a claim before three witnesses and you can hold me to it." And the old nun busied herself with her sherry.

Richard sipped his drink and looked quizzically at Joyce. "What kind of Irish whiskey is this?"

"You don't recognize it?"

"I'm glad you like it, Richard," Emtee Dempsey said, beaming. "Everyone raves about it and I have yet to get a taste of it. What have you learned from your investigation of Eileen West?"

Richard did not quite sputter, but he was obviously caught by surprise.

"Eileen West!"

"The general factotum, girl Friday, and administrative assistant to Diana Torrance."

"You figure she did it?" Richard's expression suggested that he wanted the question taken either seriously or unseriously as the sequel required.

"Then you have settled on her?"

"I don't know what the hell you're talking about and you know I don't. She was interviewed, sure, along with several dozen people connected with the Brass. She is not a suspect, no. She is not a beneficiary of the result."

"Can she account for her whereabouts when the murders occurred?"

"Sister Mary Teresa, we are seriously wondering whether we are dealing with even one murder."

"You are dealing with two."

"How do you know? Have you had a vision? The poor policeman operates under a number of constraints, things like evidence, motive, that sort of thing. Our hunches are seldom introduced as evidence in a trial. Now, I realize it is different with nuns. Given the other-worldly lives you lead, dwelling in a slum like this..."

"Irony is not your long suit, Richard."

"Is this what you asked me here for? Why not point the finger at Millie Provost? It would make about as much sense. What coach wouldn't want to murder the best player on the team?"

"I'm sure many would," Emtee Dempsey said blandly. "My question was directed at finding out what you have learned of the affair Philip Torrance was having with Eileen West."

"Tell me about it."

"Am I right in thinking that Vivian Hoy left the boat at

roughly the same time as Diana? I am. Mr. Pearson and his consort left soon after. Who spent the night with Philip Torrance? That is the question."

"You're suggesting it was Eileen West?"

"If she is his current paramour."

Richard grinned. "She was, but she ain't no more. So much for inspiration."

"Richard, just because you surprise me with an uncustomary glass of sherry you must not conclude that I am soused. I am not. I am thoroughly compos mentis and have been for over three quarters of a century."

"Well, I suggest you stick to the thirteenth century."

"The twelfth, if you don't mind. I would be more content to do so if I knew the twentieth were in good hands."

Joyce intervened. "I am going to serve supper in exactly ten minutes. How many guests do I have?"

"Not I," Katherine said, rising with a great rustle. "Frankly, I am disappointed, Sister Mary Teresa. Like Richard Moriarity, I fully expected you to pull a rabbit out of your hat."

"All in good time."

Richard drained his glass, seemed to consider asking for another, but got to his feet. "I'll run in Eileen West first thing in the morning. I am sure she'll confess as soon as I explain to her that the nuns on Walton Street have concluded she is a murderess twice over." He shook his head. "That's some way to treat one of your old students."

"Did she mention that?" Emtee Dempsey looked pleased.

"When asked about previous crimes and offenses. It's a standard question."

So Richard was able to exit on a triumphant note. It was better than a second drink. He bent and kissed Kim on the cheek before going out the door, obviously on top of the world. Well, she didn't blame him. Emtee Dempsey had a lot of nerve asking him over on false pretenses.

The old nun shook her head vigorously at the suggestion. "Not at all, Sister Kimberly. Not at all. That was an absolutely crucial visit."

On that triumphant note of her own, Emtee Dempsey settled down to the steaming risotto Joyce had put before her.

Eight

Eugene and Priscilla Evans had an apartment on the North Shore, a condominium on Siesta Key in Sarasota, and a summer home on the shore of Lake Michigan in the dunes area.

"Not a million miles from our own place," Emtee Dempsey mused.

"Seven and a half miles farther into Indiana," Joyce said, kneeling over the map she had spread on the floor of the study. The stack of copies of *Sporting News* took up most of the available surface on Emtee Dempsey's desk.

Kim came upon this scene after an enjoyable morning at the Newberry Library, the more enjoyable for seeming stolen. If she had thought of the house on Walton Street at all during those hours of hitting the books, she would have imagined Emtee Dempsey hard at work at her desk and Joyce whipping up something creative in the kitchen, the two of them enjoying the luxury of a house with no guests in it. And here they were in the study, where they had clearly spent the morning. Joyce looked up at Kim with a squinty smile. "The Evanses are neighbors of ours in Hoosierland."

"The summer place," Emtee Dempsey said, the trace of a bored drawl in her voice. She had fought to save the house on Walton Street as well as the lake home in Indiana from her sisters in religion who, after the sale of the college, began to toss money about with the abandon of John D. Rockefeller dispensing dimes. Perhaps the old nun had suspected this generosity was merely a dramatic prelude to departure from the religious life. After me, the deluge. She herself might have been motivated as much by self-interest as by loyalty to the Order of Martha and Mary. After all, if she was going to remain in the convent, there had to be a convent of sorts to remain in. That turned out to mean this house on Walton Street.

This explained Emtee Dempsey's attachment to it; her erstwhile sisters in religion had thought of it only as a toehold in the Inner City. The fight for the house in Indiana had been more purely ideological. To Emtee Dempsey's opponents it represented a sellout by the Order to the values of the middle class. "Upper middle class," Emtee Dempsey corrected them. "It is not just anyone who can afford a summer home on the Indiana shore." Salt in the wound, that remark. A red flag. But by this point Emtee Dempsey was thirsting for battle. She had known the donor of the house well. It was, predictably, an old student of hers. If she did not regard it as a personal gift, she certainly felt personally grateful for the thoughtfulness behind the donation. She did not win the struggle on the merits of her argument. By delay and rhetoric she staved off a decision until the ranks of her opponents had been decimated by defection. When the dust of battle cleared, the Order of Martha and Mary consisted of three nuns and two houses.

There was irony in the fact that Emtee Dempsey did not really like the house in Indiana. She did not dislike it either. What she could not abide was the thought of packing up and moving there for a summer sojourn. She much preferred to stay on Walton Street and continue methodically on her history of the twelfth century. But Kim and Joyce dutifully packed her off for six weeks each summer, shaming her into going by telling her she would be spoiling their chance for some fresh air and a change of scene. If the old nun dreaded anything, it was the boating Joyce insisted on. This amounted to riding the waves in a flat-bottom boat with Joyce at the oars and a terrified Emtee Dempsey grasping the sides of the boat with outstretched arms, her headdress flapping in the breeze like a captured gull. Emtee Dempsey would go naked as soon as appear in public in anything other than her religious garb. Joyce might joke that it was the only thing beside her tentlike nightgowns that fit her, but it was, Kim knew, a matter of principle with Sister Mary Teresa. And, after witnessing the almost total disintegration of the Order they had so recently joined, she and Joyce drew strength from the rock-hard solidity of Emtee Dempsey's loyalty to tradition.

Now here were Joyce and the old nun taking some strange satisfaction from learning the proximity of the Evanses' lakeshore place to their own.

"They won't come back to town," Joyce said.

"No matter, no matter that they did not respond to the suggestion. If the mountain will not go to Mohammed, Mohammed must go to the mountain. But all the others must be persuaded to be there."

Kim dropped into an armchair and looked from Joyce to Emtee Dempsey. "What are you talking about?"

"You will go ahead and prepare the way for us, Sister Kimberly. I will invite our guests for tomorrow afternoon. If only it weren't so dangerous, Richard could bring his family. The children would have so much fun on the beach."

"I doubt that Richard will trot off to Indiana at your bidding, Sister."

"Oh, he has already accepted."

"He has!"

"Imagine the police not talking to Jason Smally. Richard is just dying to talk to the Evanses and I suggested that he take up the matter at our place tomorrow. Our house in Indiana. By that time you can have it ready for guests."

"And who will our guests be?"

"Why, everyone who is involved in these dreadful murders. Richard made out a little list. Sister Joyce, do you have it?"

From the Brass there would be Norman Shire, Diana Moore Torrance, and Eileen West. The Evanses, of course. Nelson, the agent, would be there, and Pearson, though Wilma would not. For that matter, Jason Smally was not on the list either. Add Katherine Senski, Mr. Timothy Rush, their lawyer, and that was it. Counting, of course, the police and the three members of the Order of Martha and Mary.

"I suppose you will take advantage of the occasion to name the murderer of Philip Torrance and Vivian Hoy?"

"My dear, that is the whole idea of the get-together!"

Kim tried to conceal her impatience. Clearly Sister Mary Teresa was in one of her manic moods. What brazen nerve the woman had. Invite half the city of Chicago to their Indiana home so she could announce her guess as to who had murdered two people — if they had been murdered. They really should not encourage such flights of fancy. In the past, it was true, Emtee Dempsey had been lucky enough to pick the guilty one on a number of occasions, but Kim had no reason to think the old nun knew anything she herself did not, and she would no more presume to guess who had killed Philip Torrance and Vivian

Hoy on the basis of what she knew than she would swim from here to Michigan City.

"Why don't we all go to the lake house together?"

"Oh, how I wish we could," Emtee Dempsey cried. "But Mr. Rush insisted I must go with him. Naturally I cannot be alone with a man in an automobile, so Sister Joyce must wait until tomorrow too."

So it was that later that day, with the sun setting behind her, Kim directed the little VW Bug over the Chicago Skyway and then headed north on I-90. She was caught in the end-of-day exodus from Chicago and was wholly occupied with staying alive as cars and trucks rushed past her, changing lanes with the abandon of Indianapolis Speedway drivers. When she crossed into Indiana, she felt she had been shot from a gun. The traffic did not really thin out until Union Pier, when she was within minutes of the house. It was a physical relief to pull into the drive, go down a little incline, circle the house, and come to a halt before the closed doors of the triple garage. She felt she had been on the road much of the day. Actually, less than an hour had passed since she pulled away from the curb on Walton Street.

The air, when she got out of the car and stood for a moment, inhaling deeply, seemed an altogether different commodity from that with which she filled her lungs in Chicago. In the leafless branches of a tree that in summer shaded the garage a cardinal sang so sweetly Kim half believed she had made the trip for the sole purpose of hearing those pure notes on the chill Indiana air. The house was manifestly closed for the season. Nonetheless it had, despite its size, a snug, welcoming look. Kim let herself in the back door and stood listening to the sounds of the house. It was still daylight at the windows and her mind was full of a dozen happy memories of this place, but soon it would be dark. She wanted a fire in before that happened and a look of liveliness in the place. The thought she did not want to think was that she would be spending the night alone in this huge empty house on the edge of nowhere.

The first thing she did was put on a pot of coffee. The wood-box on the side porch was full and Kim transferred kindling and half a dozen small logs to the fireplace in the library. She laid the fire but did not light it. She wanted to be settled with a cup of coffee before she did that. A fire should be enjoyed from the moment of ignition. Not exactly one of the maxims of La Roche-foucauld but a truth Kim would swear by. The smell of coffee and the slight airing the house had gotten from her opening doors made her feel more at home. She went upstairs, where she had her pick of seven bedrooms. After wandering around indecisive-ly for a while, she brought her bag downstairs again. She would use what had been the maid's room behind the kitchen. She was half tempted to sleep on one of the couches in the library, but that would have made her feel like an intruder.

Light was fading at the windows when she brought in her cup of coffee. She stood holding her cup with both hands, look-ing out at the shifting colors of the lake, shades of gray and dark blue and black. How cold the water looked. She shivered when she turned away to light the fire.

There may be things more cheering than a fire, but at the moment Kim could not think of one. She sat with her feet curled under her on the couch opposite the fire and took from her purse a note Emtee Dempsey had given her before leaving.

Emtee Dempsey had handed her an envelope, sealed. Open-ing it, Kim was surprised to find a letter.

"Dear Sister Kimberly," Emtee Dempsey began in her beautiful hand. "You are now safely ensconced in our house on the shores of Lake Michigan in Indiana, out of harm's way. I can now tell you that part of the reason for sending you on ahead is to exempt you from any criticism my actions may elicit from the police and from your brother Richard in particular. I will say no more of that for now. In any case, that is only part of the reason why I wanted you to be there. The Evanses have of course agreed to come to our place tomorrow afternoon. I want you to contact them today, after you get comfortable, something I expect you have done before opening this note. Ask them if you could drop by their place for a chat. Use whatever is required to have a face-to-face conversation with them. The telephone will not do. I could do that from here. You will tell them that you feel some apprehension about tomorrow because I have announced that at the get-together in our lake place I will reveal the murderer of Philip Torrance and Vivian Hoy. Suggest that you fear for my good sense. (Do try to be convincing; you acted in several plays at the college, if I remember, and you should be able to dissemble enough to convince the Evanses.) Of course this will not quell their curiosity as to what I know. Tell them the following and attend carefully to their reactions: (1) I know that in a rage he threw a paperweight at Philip Torrance; (2) I know that he and his wife spent the night on their boat in Belmont Harbor the night Philip Torrance was killed and I shall inform the police of this; (3) I know of their plotting with Norman Shire on the Jersey Jills matter; (4) Vivian Hoy's diary has come into my possession. You may mention these things in any order you wish and with whatever prefatory disclaimers seem appropriate, but I shall expect an exact account of their reactions. Their reactions — hers as well as his. With love and devotion in Our Lord and Our Lady, Sister Mary Teresa Dempsey, M.& M."

Not pitching the page into the fire did more to build Kim's character than it reflected the one she already had. She had been sent away! Gotten out from under Emtee Dempsey's feet. She was on a largely diversionary errand, that was more than clear.

She got up from the couch and paced angrily up and down

the room. Three of the four walls were covered with books, other people's books; it was like the study on Walton Street. Many of these books had come with the house, however. Novels of the late forties and early fifties, popular history, lots of sets looking largely untouched. Her coffee was cold. She went to the kitchen for a refill, for a mad moment thought of making a drink. There must be some stale cigarettes somewhere, cached and forgotten by Joyce. She brushed the thought away. It would have been too much to call it a temptation. Its appeal was as a species of long-distance nose-thumbing at Emtee Dempsey. What on earth was the old girl up to?

The sound of the ringing phone lifted the hair on her head. The realization that only her sisters on Walton Street knew she was here sent her scurrying to the phone.

"Hello! Then you are there. That is Sister Kimberly, is it not? This is Priscilla Evans. We have had the most curious call from Chicago."

"Hello, Mrs. Evans."

"I understand we're neighbors. What an extraordinary thing."

"Can you stop by tomorrow afternoon?"

"Such a mysterious invitation."

"You don't know the half of it."

"Oh."

"Didn't Sister Mary Teresa tell you? She has announced she is going to name the murderer tomorrow afternoon."

"You're not serious."

"The important thing is that she is. Of course I don't for a minute think she can do it. Oh, she could name someone, but will it be the murderer?"

"Maybe she does know," Mrs. Evans said tentatively.

Kim, not without morose delectation, told Priscilla Evans that Emtee Dempsey's mind was not all it used to be and her invitation simply one of those obsessions that gripped her now in her waning days. This disloyal remark was all the sweeter on the tongue because Mrs. Evans obviously did not believe her. The prospect of the morrow's revelation lifted no weight from her heart. Kim remarked that it was a relief to be able to speak frankly. Priscilla suggested Kim come over. Now. And Kim agreed. There was a somewhat triumphant tone in Priscilla Evans's voice as she gave Kim detailed directions to the Evanses' lakeshore home.

One of the advantages of seeing the Evanses' place was that Kim felt that in the future she would be less troubled by scruples about their own. A series of terraces brought the eye of the visitor to the glass house overlooking the lake and an asphalt drive brought her to the open double doors framing the Evanses. Kim felt she was being adopted when the couple took her hands and led her inside. The sunken living room was comfortably plush. Eugene Evans, hands stuffed into the side pockets of his gray suede jacket, asked if she would like a drink. Priscilla had picked up a frosted glass from the coffee table and now took a sip, as if in encouragement of Kim's thirst. Kim refused and Evans sat down with obvious relief.

"Now, what is this nonsense about Sister Mary Teresa?"

It was difficult to avoid self-consciousness during the next forty-five minutes. Kim decided to read the points from Emtee Dempsey's letter, inviting the sympathy of the Evanses, citing them as the basis for her suspicion that the old nun was heading rapidly around the bend. But all the while she watched carefully the couple's reactions.

She had the impression that Priscilla's whole concern was to divert her from her husband's reaction. He, in turn, registered annoyed disdain at (1), unfeigned alarm at (2), indifference to (3), a quick glance at Priscilla at (4).

"How could she possibly know what nights we spent on our boat?"

"That boy," Priscilla said, the words escaping her like air from a balloon.

"Jason Smally," Kim said.

"We could have gone to the harbor that morning," Evans said. He seemed to be thinking aloud.

"And left because of the fuss over Philip Torrance?"

"Yes!" cried Priscilla, and Kim felt cruel for having offered her this false relief.

"The body hadn't been discovered yet," Evans said, his voice taking on a warning tone.

"We saw it and left." His eyes narrowed and his ears seemed to move back on his head. It was as if Evans had told his wife to shut up.

"You say she is going to make an announcement. To whom?"

"Isn't that like her not to mention it." Whereupon Kim rattled off the names. She was beginning to enjoy this. She wished she had accepted a drink. Well, a Coke. And then she felt bad about going through this charade. The Evanses were reluctant to let her go, but Kim said she had to get the house ready for the following day.

When she drove away, the couple was once again framed in the open double doors of their lovely glass house. Their manner was not what it had been when she arrived.

Back in their own house, she put through a call to the house on Walton Street, but the phone rang and rang, unanswered. Emtee Dempsey might ignore a ringing phone by the hour, but Joyce could not.

She sat next to the phone, sipping her cool coffee, looking and feeling forlorn and abandoned. It was one of those moments when she could not avoid thinking of the future when Sister Mary Teresa would no longer be with them and the Order of Martha and Mary might consist of only Joyce and herself. The prospect was bottomlessly depressing. How could two young women claim to be a religious order? As long as Sister Mary Teresa was alive, the cardinal would leave well enough alone, but when she was out of the picture, he might very well accept the view, pressed by some of those who had left, that the Order of Martha and Mary no longer existed. I will become a Trappistine, Kim thought, but it was a romantic dream, like the thought of making herself a drink and lighting up a cigarette.

There was a TV dinner in the freezer of the kitchen refrigerator and some diet pop beneath the sink. The combination was like camping out, but Kim had lost all desire to make herself an elaborate meal. Was she trying to punish Emtee Dempsey by denying herself? Maybe, but she would be punishing herself if she insisted on cooking a big meal. She turned on the oven and put some pop into the refrigerator. The radio? She hesitated, then turned on WBBM, a station devoted to constant news, weather, and traffic reports. Five minutes of cheery accounts of disasters around the globe was all she could take. There was a tape deck in the living room. Kim put on some Brahms, setting the volume so high that the whole house pulsed with soothing music. It was necessary to have lights on. She had pulled only the library drapes, so there was no need to worry about that. The library windows looked out on the lake, over a steep cliff. It was absurdly easy to imagine unseen observers outside in the dark. Kim laughed aloud to exorcise the thought. The sound of her laughter was thin and unconvincing. Thank God for the music.

Feeling a bit like Joyce, she sat at the kitchen table with her cup of warmed-over coffee and tried to imagine what Emtee Dempsey was up to. The old nun had put herself on the line when she said she knew who had murdered Philip Torrance and Vivian Hoy.

Two nights before, the Chicago Brass, a team that had almost overcome the loss of Vivian Hoy, lost a game in Denver that put them out of the play-off picture. Their season was done. Unless they picked up some players, unless they found a star to replace Vivian, the franchise, in Joyce's estimate, was in danger. Recalling that remark, remembering the stacks of *Sporting News* on Emtee Dempsey's desk, Kim tried to imagine what line the old nun was pursuing. Reviewing the events of the past weeks was more confusing than enlightening.

Diana Moore Torrance had come to visit her old teacher to tell her that her marriage was in danger, that she had decided to leave her husband. Emtee Dempsey had sent her away with a message as Delphic as any oracle's. Shortly after, Diana was on their doorstep again. The body of her husband had been found floating in Belmont Harbor. The story she told of the previous night despite her denials, made her the prime suspect in her husband's death. Typically, Emtee Dempsey had offered her old student refuge, dissembling when the police, i.e. Richard, came calling, seemingly believing every word Diana told her, though claiming later that she had doubted her from the beginning. The old nun seemed then to be casting Vivian Hoy for the part of murderess and sought some plausible motive for the deed. So she had sent Kim on a visit to the athlete under the guise of woman journalist and the only immediate result had been that Vivian rightly thought Kim two-faced. Then Vivian Hoy too was found dead. Had that been in any way the result of Kim's call? That was the kind of speculation Emtee Dempsey rejected with real anger.

"Our roles in divine providence go far beyond our own intentions or anything we can be held responsible for. Her death occurred after your visit, not because of it, at least not in any causal sense that involves you. We are creatures, Sister. More than pawns on God's chessboard, but partial pawns at least. Be humble."

It was best not to ask for any elaboration on such remarks,

as the result was likely to be of lecture length. Emtee Dempsey said that all those years in the classroom had programmed her to fifty-minute discourses, and one prompted her into action at his or her own peril. In any case, there were now two bodies and the tragicomic interlude of Norman Shire claiming to have killed Vivian. It had exasperated Katherine that both Diana and Shire had sought to be blamed for crimes they could not possibly have committed. So what else did they know? That Eileen West was having or had had an affair with Philip Torrance. (Richard had found proof positive of this.) That Pearson had flown north from Florida to enjoy a night of dalliance with Wilma, a harbor tramp who nonetheless had had the civic sense to confess their presence on the *Brass Cupcake* the night Philip Torrance was killed.

How from these facts Emtee Dempsey could claim to know who had murdered Philip Torrance and Vivian Hoy Kim did not see. It had been easy to play the role with the Evanses Emtee Dempsey assigned her because Kim really did think the old nun had overreached herself. She would say wild things, pull some stunt, hope that the guilty party, if he or she was in the room, would oblige with a confession. And if they did not? It would be a long quiet drive back to the house on Walton Street.

The more Kim thought of it, the less she looked forward to the following afternoon. Emtee Dempsey's letter suggested she thought Evans was the murderer. Was that even possible? Why not? A blow on the head and pitching someone into the water. It was child's play, when she thought about it. Vivian? An overdose administered by someone else called for cunning and stealth, not superior strength.

Kim did not believe a word of it.

She ate her TV dinner and drank her diet soft drink. Brahms ran out and she put on Bach. Stay with the Bs; it was the only thing she remembered from Music Appreciation 1. The ecstatic precision of music, the haunting melody of the Air for the G string, carried Kim along and the evening passed swiftly. She built up a fire, took a massive novel called *Anthony Adverse* from the shelves, and was soon half caught up in its incredible adventures. A scene or two struck her as remarkably risqué for the thirties, not that she was an expert on the matter. But it helped to keep from her mind the puzzling speculation that had plagued her before supper.

The fire died down, the tape ended, the book grew boring. Bedtime. Lying in the dark, staring at the ceiling, she assured herself that Emtee Dempsey did not have a notion in the world who the killer was. This rebellious thought lulled her gently into sleep.

During the night it was noisier than it ever was in Chicago, and Walton Street kept busy until the wee hours. But here there was the wind off the lake and the odd creakings and groans of the house, and a steady distant but all-too-audible sound of planes descending toward O'Hare. Kim awoke to this non-urban racket and for more than half an hour attended to it. Finally, to the half-real, half-imagined sound of the lake endlessly rocking in the huge basin created by the passage of a glacier eons ago, she slid once more into sleep.

Nine

When Kim woke up the following morning it was with the pleasant expectancy that she had arisen on Christmas mornings as a girl. Presents, surprises, peace and good will. The moment was short-lived when she recalled the object of her expectancy now.

It was already after ten. In a few hours would come the moment of truth and, as Joyce might have said, they would learn who was the matador and who was the bull. Or what.

After ten? Ye gods! She still had to get the house presentable for guests.

In the kitchen she made tea, put in two slices of toast, and, nibbling and sipping, made a circuit of the house assessing the dimensions of her task. There was no need to worry about the second floor, and on the main floor the large sitting room would be ample enough to accommodate Emtee Dempsey's guests more than comfortably.

During the next two hours Kim knew the joys of housework. She vacuumed, she dusted, she washed dishes and glasses, she made sure there would be plenty of ice. Refreshments? The cupboard over the refrigerator was filled with various bottles of liquor, Scotch, bourbon, gin. And there were wines as well. Beer?

She found several twelve-can cartons in the basement and put the contents of one into the refrigerator, thinking of the cops Richard might bring along as she did so. Immediately she pushed thoughts of her brother from her mind. If this afternoon turned into a fiasco, he would feel more than vindicated for past embarrassment at the hands of Sister Mary Teresa. Only the last feat, or defeat, counted. If the old nun made a fool of herself today, no one would remember all the times when she had solved murders Richard and his colleagues had been unable to.

It wasn't fair. She dialed the Walton Street number again, but receiving no answer meant nothing. Joyce and Emtee Dempsey would be on their way now, sitting in the back seat of Mr. Rush's car.

By one o'clock Kim had the house ready for guests and five minutes later the first one arrived. Norman Shire. He did not seem sober and she told him so.

"My appearances are seldom deceiving. Is that the roar of the surf I hear? I should go down and walk upon the water."

"You'd do better drinking it."

"I will take a cup of coffee."

He took it into the study, put it carefully on the table beside his chair, and fell asleep. There was the sound of a horn outside and Kim ran to the front door to see Mr. Rush's large black and very shiny car whisk up the drive and come to a stop at the entrance. Unlike the Evanses on the previous day, she ran to greet the occupants of the car.

Rush wisely stayed behind the wheel, ready to move the car when he had discharged his passengers. Joyce hopped out, gave Kim her cross-eyed lolling-tongue look, and said, "You get the other door."

She was suggesting that Kim open the opposite back door and push while Joyce pulled so that they could get Sister Mary Teresa and her enormous headdress out of the car. This was achieved with much huffing and puffing and looks of injured dignity from the recipient of their help, but soon they had Sister Mary Teresa upright and none the worse for wear on the driveway. The car moved away noiselessly. Emtee Dempsey looked at the house with frowning appraisal.

"Who is here?"

"Here come the Evanses," Joyce said, and indeed, the couple was approaching on foot up the driveway, having left their car on the turnaround in front of the garages. Evans leaned forward as if he were mounting an incline and, since the drive was level, the explanation seemed to be overweening curiosity. He came directly to Emtee Dempsey and put out his hand. She took it in both of hers and greeted him and his wife warmly. Had Evans just been exonerated, or had Emtee Dempsey given him a Judas kiss?

Richard came next, accompanied by Gleason and O'Connell, whose look made Kim feel that she and not Emtee Dempsey was Judas here. Within twenty minutes everyone had come and it was a relief to learn that Sister Mary Teresa had told them all the purpose of the meeting. It had been impossible for Kim to speak to Emtee Dempsey about her visit to the Evanses.

"I'm looking forward to this," Nelson said with a smile, and Diana tugged him on into the living room. Eileen wore a wine red suit and her hair seemed even shorter than before. She is more attractive than she was as a girl, Kim thought, despite the brittle quality, almost hardness. Not that Kim was criticizing. Eileen impressed her. Perhaps her hardness was the price a woman paid to make it in the business world. Yet, Katherine

Senski, for all her competence and success, retained an unmistakable femininity.

"Glory be to God," she murmured when she saw all the people Emtee Dempsey had summoned.

Another twenty minutes went by before the tableau Emtee Dempsey wanted had established itself in the massive sitting room of the vacation house. Before they went in, Emtee Dempsey nodded through Kim's account of her visit to the Evanses, asking no questions. Katherine settled herself in a leather chair and surveyed with commanding condescension the others in the room. Only a friend could detect how nervous Katherine was. Did anyone have faith in Emtee Dempsey other than Emtee Dempsey herself? The Evanses, any reassurance they might have derived from Emtee Dempsey's greeting gone, now sat side by side on one of the couches that flanked the fireplace, looking aggrieved. Across from them Norman Shire sipped from the massive Bloody Mary Joyce had provided him. Nelson was perched on the arm of Diana's chair, his eyes darting from face to face, excited anticipation in his manner. In the hall outside, O'Connell and Gleason lounged. Kim hoped that Emtee Dempsey could deliver what she promised — the stage was certainly set and failure would be public and devastating.

Richard called them to order. "I am Lieutenant Moriarity of the Chicago Police and I am here, like most of you, because Sister Mary Teresa invited me. Despite the fact that the Cook County coroner is inclined to think the deaths of Philip Torrance and Vivian Hoy may both have been accidental, our hostess insists that they were murdered."

"And I know who murdered them," Emtee Dempsey added, much as she might have corrected a grammatical error in Richard's remarks. The old nun sat in front, a teacher before her class, and she looked around at them with arch amusement. If she felt the least bit of apprehension, Kim could not detect it.

"I'm glad you said that." Richard did not look glad. "I dissociate myself in advance from any accusations that may be made here on the basis of hunches and intuitions or whatever. It is my settled professional opinion that Sister Mary Teresa knows no more than I do and that she is bluffing."

Sister Mary Teresa laughed a tinkling little laugh. "Lieutenant Moriarity is always piqued when the solution to a puzzle is at hand. But let's get down to business. Let me review the events of the past weeks."

Emtee Dempsey settled into her high-backed brocade chair, elbows on its arms, fingertips touching, her feet barely reaching the floor. Her eyes closed meditatively behind her rimless spectacles. Her narrative was succinct, dramatic, and as far as Kim could see, complete.

Several weeks ago, Diana Moore Torrance paid a visit on her old history professor. They had not seen each other for twenty years, but of course Sister Mary Teresa recognized her immediately and had dozens of vivid memories of Diana as a college girl. Emtee Dempsey opened her eyes and looked at those gathered before her as if to surprise some skeptical reaction. But there was none and she resumed.

"I break no confidence now if I say that Diana's description of her marriage to Philip Torrance was grim. She had decided to leave him, despite the great success the two of them had known as owners of the Chicago Brass."

"Part owners," Priscilla Evans said.

"Part owners," Emtee Dempsey agreed. "Mr. and Mrs. Evans also have a share, as does Norman Shire."

The sportswriter's lips were red from his drink. He nodded, bowed, actually, and for a moment Kim feared that he would continue forward and somersault across the room.

"Diana had decided to leave her husband and she came to me with this decision. Why? To be dissuaded? I don't think so.

To gain approval? I think not. Perhaps she wanted to hear herself say it aloud and find out if she really meant it. In any case, she left as unresolved as she came. A few days later she was again on my doorstep, this time because her husband's body had been found floating in Belmont Harbor."

"And you gave her sanctuary," Richard said.

"What a lovely way of putting it. Yes, we gave her sanctuary. We were repaid with the most preposterous imaginable account of how her husband had died. Diana . . . Well, there is no need to repeat her imaginative story. The net effect of it was to draw suspicion on herself, but safely, since she could not possibly have killed her husband."

"I could have killed him," Diana said quietly.

"So could I." Norman Shire spoke with the deliberateness of one unsure his words would come out unslurred.

"But Diana did not kill him," Emtee Dempsey said. "On the night he died, Philip Torrance was on his boat in Belmont Harbor. He had remained there in a rage after both his wife and Vivian Hoy had left him there alone. Other guests had also gone. It might seem a reasonable assumption that Philip Torrance remained alone. Here was a man who, after years of philandering, had told his wife he was leaving her. His hope was to marry Vivian Hoy."

"When she left the boat with me that night, I think Phil realized Vivian was leaving him for good."

Emtee Dempsey nodded. "I assume from what I have heard of him that he was not a man likely to sulk on his boat alone."

"How do you know when Vivian Hoy left the boat?" Richard was impatient.

"She returned to her building at 2:45," Emtee Dempsey said sweetly. "Am I correct, Mr. Evans?"

Evans and his wife had been listening to the old nun with somewhat disdainful curiosity. He lurched slightly at Emtee

Dempsey's question and his face beneath his silver hair grew slowly pink.

"I have no idea when Vivian returned to her apartment that night."

"I was referring to when she left the *Brass Cupcake.* Isn't that the name of the Torrance boat?"

"I have no idea when she left the *Brass Cupcake,*" Eugene Evans said, annoyed.

"You and your wife were on your own boat that night, were you not?"

Evans looked at her steadily for several moments without speaking and it was his wife who answered. "We slept on the boat that night, yes. At the time you mention, we would have been dead to the world."

"And so soon would Philip Torrance be," Emtee Dempsey said. "Were the two of you ever guests on Philip Torrance's boat?"

"It was not Philip's boat," Diana said sharply. "It was *our* boat."

"On the Torrance boat," Emtee Dempsey amended.

Priscilla Evans looked closely at Sister Mary Teresa. "Are you a sailor?"

"What is the point of your question?"

"I wonder if you know what it is like at a marina. You speak of being guests. Things are far less formal than the word suggests. People stop by one another's boats all the time. Such visiting is seldom by invitation."

"You mean people paddle about from boat to boat in their dinghies?"

Mrs. Evans smiled. "You see, you have it all wrong. It's not a matter of prowling around among other people's boats. You notice a friend, wave, call to each other, perhaps visit."

Emtee Dempsey nodded, an avid and grateful pupil. "Did you visit the Torrance boat the night Philip Torrance was murdered?"

The Evanses shook their heads in unison.

"I understand that the Torrance boat was anchored to a buoy and was not in a slip."

"That's right."

"And your own?"

"We were not in a slip either."

"How near the Torrance boat were you anchored?"

The Evanses looked at each other. He said to her, "Several boats away?"

"That's right," she told him.

"Were you aware of the fact that Philip Torrance was on his boat that night?"

"I wasn't," Mrs. Evans said.

"Nor I," said her husband. "Not until the following day, that is."

"When you learned that he had drowned?"

"That's right."

"You left your boat very early the following morning. In fact, only minutes before Jason Smally discovered the body. And neither of you noticed him floating in the water."

"If we had, we would have reported it," Eugene Evans said in frosty tones.

It seemed to Kim that her visit to the Evanses had enabled them to deflect all suspicion from themselves.

"Yes." Emtee Dempsey brought her fingertips together and closed her eyes. Suddenly they snapped open. "Is everybody comfortable? Can Sister Joyce get you something to drink?"

"I'll have another of these," Norman Shire said, waggling his empty glass.

"Anyone else?"

"It is not yet three in the afternoon," Eugene Evans said.

"You see. I am as uninformed about entertaining as I am about yacht basins."

"I'll have Scotch and water," Nelson said, smiling defiantly at Evans. "You don't even drink, Gene. What do you know?"

Katherine Senski decided she wanted a glass of wine. Richard asked for a beer and Diana got up to help Joyce. "I'll make my own, Sister."

Kim said to Eileen, "Anything for you?"

"What is this, a party?"

"Not for someone it isn't. More like a final repast."

"She's actually going to tell us who killed Phil and Vivian?"

"That's what she says."

"I don't believe it."

"There's only one way to find out."

"I wouldn't leave for the world. What kind of wine do you have?"

"Come on with me."

They went into the kitchen to help Joyce. Like Diana, Eileen seemed glad to get away from the sitting room.

"She seems to think it was the Evanses," Diana said to Kim, shaking her head. "That's impossible."

Kim shrugged her shoulders. "Don't ask me. I'm a spectator like everyone else."

"I agree with your brother," Eileen said. "I think she's bluffing."

"After yesterday, I can believe you," Joyce said.

"What about yesterday?" Diana asked.

"It's a long story. We'd better go back. Give me a hand with these."

There were several murmuring conversations going on in the living room when they came in. Richard and Katherine conversed behind the reporter's gloved hand. Nelson was on the arm of the Evanses' couch now listening to Mrs. Evans while her husband looked straight ahead as if the exchange had nothing to do with him. Norman Shire was turned toward the door and looked relieved at the appearance of the drinks. Sister Mary

Teresa seemed lost in meditation: steepled hands, closed eyes, her mouth an expressionless line.

"We're ready," Katherine said when everyone was once more settled.

The old nun opened her eyes. "Vivian Hoy learned of the death of her employer when Sister Kimberly called on her the next day. You are convinced that the news caught her by surprise, are you not, Sister?"

"At the time I thought she was acting," Kim said.

"But you changed your mind?"

"Yes."

"Sometime later she too was killed. Dead of a fatal combination of liquor and drugs, neither of which she used. Isn't that right, Mr. Nelson?"

"Everyone knows that. She had no vices."

"She smoked," Eileen whispered, and Sister Mary Teresa turned to her.

"That's right. She smoked."

"I take the blame for that," Norman Shire said, and he seemed ready to cry.

"Do you have anything you'd like to add, Mr. Nelson?"

The agent looked startled, then reproachful. "What do you mean?"

"You know what I mean."

In the ensuing silence, the object of everyone's curiosity, Nelson squirmed nervously. The look he gave Diana was that of a test pilot just before he closes the cockpit canopy. "Okay," he said finally. "Okay. I was a damned fool to tell you about it in the first place, so I guess I have this coming."

"I have not broken your confidence," Emtee Dempsey said.

"Oh, hell no." Nelson addressed Richard. "I didn't tell you this and I should have. I was the one who discovered Vivian was dead. I should have reported it and I didn't."

Richard pushed away from the wall. "Yes, you should have. Why didn't you? Tell me about it."

Richard moved to impose himself between Sister Mary Teresa and Nelson, taking over, but the old nun clucked at him.

"Richard, be patient a little longer. You have yet to hear the interesting thing. Mr. Nelson, tell Lieutenant Moriarity the disposition of the body when you discovered it."

While Nelson told, in sentences that sounded telegraphic they were so reluctantly spoken, how he had found the body of Vivian Hoy, Richard returned to his post beside the fireplace.

"That isn't the way she was found," he said when Nelson was finished. "She was found in her bed."

"Then someone moved her."

"Why?"

"I don't know."

"Did it occur to you to move her?"

"Of course not. It was horrible, finding her like that. I just wanted to get the hell out of there."

"The question is, Mr. Nelson, was she dead when you got there?"

"If you're suggesting I killed my own client, you're crazy. Without her I was next to nothing."

"*Next* to nothing?" Priscilla Evans asked in a stage whisper.

"Maybe you insured her," Evans said.

"Insured her?"

"Of course. To protect your investment. For injury. For life. It would only be good business."

Sister Mary Teresa said, "Mr. Evans, did the team have an insurance policy on Vivian Hoy?"

"Certainly," Diana said. "Eugene insisted on it. We insured her legs separately. And we had a life policy on her too."

"That's interesting. For how much was her life insured?"

"Five million dollars," Diana said matter-of-factly.

"Five million dollars!"

Evans cleared his throat. "That is the amount we had contracted to pay her over the next ten years, and we would have had to pay it whether or not she was able to play. It would have been folly not to insure such an obligation."

Sister Mary Teresa said what was by now clear to everybody in the room. "In short, Norman Shire, Diana Torrance, and the Evanses will shortly be the recipients of five million dollars in compensation for the death of Vivian Hoy."

Evans said, "If you're talking insurance, let's get to Phil. He must have been insured too. How about it, Diana? What do you stand to make out of Phil's death?"

"That's none of your business."

"I take it that means the team had no insurance policy on Philip Torrance?" Sister Mary Teresa said.

"What on earth for?" Priscilla Evans asked.

"Philip Torrance was insured for half a million dollars," Richard said. "With Amalgamated Life. Their investigators have contacted us."

"The manner of death affects the policy, I suppose."

Richard said, "Sister, I am no insurance expert, but I can assure you that if Philip Torrance was murdered no insurance company is going to hand over any money until they are convinced they are not rewarding a criminal."

"If?" Priscilla Evans turned to look at Richard.

Emtee Dempsey clearly liked this line of inquiry. "I imagine the same would apply to Vivian Hoy's policy. If the owners of the team were responsible for her death, they would be unable to collect on it?"

Richard made a face. "I suppose. I don't know. Look, Sister, I didn't come here to make guesses about insurance payoffs. You say you know who killed two people. Okay, who is it?"

The old nun nodded. "Very well. But first a question for

you. Yesterday you wasted a good deal of time following me around Chicago. I hope you enjoyed the boat ride and view from the Sears Tower."

"Is this another run-around?"

"Another?"

"You know what I mean."

"Tell me what you mean. Why do you say that I gave you the run-around yesterday? What did you think Mr. Rush and I were doing?"

Richard laughed a bitter laugh. "You were supposed to have a rendezvous with the murderer."

"Ah. Exactly. Wonderful." Sister Mary Teresa stood and opened her arms wide. "That settles it. I know the murderer."

"Who the hell is it?"

Sister Mary Teresa had been moving to her left, toward Kim. As she drew near, she seemed to stumble and, as she fell forward, she grasped Eileen West's arm for support. Eileen tried to help the old nun regain her balance.

"Are you all right, Sister?"

"Tell them, young lady. I would rather they hear it from your lips than from mine."

Eileen looked at the nun with a bright false smile. "What are you talking about?"

"My dear, you informed the police about my supposed rendezvous, did you not? The poor things spent much of the day following me around the city. Richard Moriarity then accuses me of giving him a run-around.

"You have made all your enemies rich, Eileen. Don't you realize that? Diana and Mr. Nelson will have half a million for Philip and their share of the five million for Vivian Hoy. All you got was revenge."

"Once Phil and I had a thing, I don't deny that. Everyone knew it. Even Diana." And Eileen looked defiantly at her employer.

"The only thing I didn't know was that it was over."

"Oh, it was over," Eileen said. "Phil had finally figured out a way to fulfill his dream. He couldn't be an athlete but he could marry one if it was a woman. And Vivian was very much a woman. The only problem was that she loved money more than love."

Priscilla Evans spoke with awed certainty. "You were on the boat that night, Eileen. You were there after Diana and Vivian took the dinghy to shore. I saw them go in and twenty minutes later I saw you rowing out to the *Brass Cupcake*."

"Not me, you didn't."

Richard said, "You left your building that night, Miss West. You took your car from the garage at two-thirty A.M."

"What does that prove?"

"That you took your car from the garage at two-thirty A.M. Where did you go?"

Eileen's eyes might have been scanning some inner screen, looking for a plausible reply. "For a ride. I wanted some air."

"Did Philip Torrance call and invite you to his boat?"

"Ha!"

Emtee Dempsey said, "Eileen, you had motive. You resented the way Philip Torrance had cast you aside as he had cast aside so many others. You must have considered yourself different and it was cruel to learn that he did not agree. If you resented Philip, you must have hated Vivian."

"We were friends, Vivian and I."

"Friends."

"And anyway, the motive you give me was shared by others. As you said, I was not the only woman in Chicago who had..." Eileen glanced at Diana and did not finish the sentence.

"You also had opportunity. You are the only one who was both on the boat and in Vivian's apartment at the times of the murders."

"I was not! They were there at the harbor, on their boat." Eileen pointed a painted finger at the Evanses.

"Yes, they were. And they had motive to kill Philip Torrance, motive and opportunity. They had neither in the case of Vivian."

"So they killed Philip and he killed her."

He was Nelson. The agent, holding an unlit cigarette in one hand and Diana's hand in his other, shook his head. "Me kill Vivian? That's crazy."

"I thought of that," Emtee Dempsey said. "Mr. Nelson was in many ways a puzzling figure. He visited me on Walton Street with a flattering but unconvincing story that he was an admirer of my work. I asked myself where he could have learned about me. The aroma of his cigar gave a clue. It was the same smell I had detected on Diana Torrance the first time she came to visit me. It suggested a liaison that, in the event, is evident."

Diana freed her hand from Nelson's but did not resist when once again he took it.

Evans said, "Were you at the harbor that night, Nelson?"

"No."

"But you were in Vivian Hoy's apartment," Eileen said. She was not as panicky as she had been; she seemed almost to be enjoying the conversation.

"As were you," Emtee Dempsey reminded her. "It was you who discovered the body, Eileen."

"Exactly." Eileen shrugged at Richard. "That will hardly come as news to anyone."

Joyce, who had not returned to the room after the break for drinks, appeared in the doorway and nodded at Emtee Dempsey, who said, "Bring them in, Sister."

A moment later Jason Smally and Wilma stood there, looking around the room. Silence fell. And then Wilma smiled.

"Hi," she said. She was addressing Eileen West.

"Do you know this woman?" Emtee Dempsey asked Wilma.

"Sure."

"In what capacity?"

Richard spoke, "Do you get coke from her, Wilma?"

"She's the one who introduced me to it," the girl said, and her voice was suddenly angry. "When she used to be at the harbor a lot."

Emtee Dempsey said, "Richard, all this is relevant, of course, but let me carry on, will you? Wilma, on the night Philip Torrance died..."

"She did it." And Wilma pointed at Eileen. "After his wife and Vivian left, Phil gave her a call and out she came. George and I left, but I heard them arguing from George's boat—she wanted things the way they had been. He laughed. And then he stopped. I saw her dump him over the side."

And that was when Eileen came at Wilma, moving so swiftly across the room that no one could stop her. She grabbed the girl by the hair, wrestled her to the rug, and began to bang her head against the floor. It took Kim and Richard and Joyce almost a minute to get Eileen off Wilma.

Richard, flustered and out of breath, gasped, "I'm not going to continue this here. Bring her along." So Gleason and O'Connell took the struggling, weeping, hysterical Eileen West and led her away after Richard.

"I want another drink," Norman Shire said, his voice oddly sober.

Everybody wanted a drink, even those who had disdained the offer previously. Sister Mary Teresa herself took a bit of sherry.

"I don't know what we're celebrating," she said, trying to look stern. "What a dreadful thing. That girl was a student of mine."

"So was I," Diana said. "And you all but accused me of killing my husband."

"We drink to you, Sister Mary Teresa," Eugene Evans said. "How did you suspect her?"

"Several things." Emtee Dempsey sipped her sherry. "First was recalling an old contretemps when Eileen West was a college student. Second was Vivian Hoy's diary."

"Diary? What diary?"

Nelson said, "I'm glad you didn't bring that up when the police were here."

"Oh, I'll be passing it on to them."

Kim said, "I don't recall any mention of Eileen in the diary."

"Neither do I," said Joyce.

Sister Mary Teresa beamed. "I didn't suppose you had. But she is mentioned all right. Many times."

For the moment that is all she would say, and neither Kim nor Joyce pressed her on it. It seemed best to allow the old nun to enjoy her moment of triumph, to wallow in the praise lavished on her by Norman Shire, Diana, the Evanses, and Nelson. She deserved it. And not the least benefit of what she had done was that Richard would be placated.

"You have outdone yourself," Katherine said. "And I have not the least idea how you did it."

"It was nothing," Sister Mary Teresa protested. "Nothing."

She sounded a bit like God on the Seventh Day.

Ten

Katherine left, the Evanses left, Norman Shire left, but Diana and Nelson remained. The agent had been drinking straight-bourbon since Eileen West had been taken away, and he looked as if he could not keep himself from smiling. For that matter, Diana seemed to have shed ten years. There was a girlishness about her when she took Nelson's glass away for a refill.

"I'll get drunk," he warned.

"You're entitled."

Joyce went with Diana. Nelson leaned forward in his chair, his hands falling between his knees. He looked almost beseechingly at Sister Mary Teresa, but still wore his idiot grin.

"I thought it was her," he said, and his grin widened. "I thought it was Diana."

"Is that why you moved Vivian Hoy's body?"

"How did you know that?"

"Doubtless you thought it would look more like suicide if she was found in bed."

"You're guessing, aren't you?"

"But accurately, no?"

"Don't tell Diana what I thought."

"What did you think?" Diana swept into the room bearing Nelson's bourbon as if it were a reward.

Emtee Dempsey said, "Perhaps you should explain to Mr. Nelson why you told such a wild story about what had happened on the *Brass Cupcake.*"

"It doesn't matter now." Diana, having given Nelson his drink, sat beside him on the couch.

"Diana, you owe it to Sister Kimberly and Joyce. Unlike myself, they took seriously what you said about being on the boat with your husband and Vivian Hoy and a couple you called the Pearsons. Please tell them who you thought you were protecting with that story."

"Me?" Nelson's grin grew wider.

"I was sure you had done it."

"I thought it was you!"

Diana squealed like a teen-ager and then the two of them were trading excited stories of their suspicions and fears and what they had done to deflect suspicion from the other. Eventually Emtee Dempsey called a halt to it and the happy couple took their leave. It was a macabre thought that it had been the death of Diana's husband that had brought her and the agent to the realization that they were more than friends.

It was eight o'clock when the Sisters got back to Walton Street, having stopped at a McDonald's on the way home. This was meant as a treat for Joyce, but she didn't take it that way.

"Okay," Joyce said. "I want to know where Eileen West is mentioned in Vivian Hoy's diary."

"Surely you must have figured it out by now."

"I have not figured it out by now. I will not have figured it out by then. Tell me."

"Sister Kimberly?"

"I give up."

Emtee Dempsey sighed. "All right. Get the diary. Let's go into my study."

When the old nun was seated at her desk, the diary open before her and Joyce on one side and Kim on the other, she pointed at an entry. "PT-109 and I at BH. WW furious. Ha. Or ho. WWho."

"What's it mean?" Joyce asked.

"She was with Philip Torrance on his boat and someone referred to as WW is furious. Now look at the last entry in the diary. '2 gls yesterday in Bluesville. PT-109 dead.' She scored two goals the previous day in St. Louis. There is an asterisk — *, the usual sign for the end of an entry. Then the final line. 'WW called and coming over.' That must have been written on the day of her own death and WW was the last one to see her alive."

"And WW is Eileen West?"

"That's right. Westward."

"How did you guess?" Joyce asked.

"Guess?"

"Deduce," Kim said. She was dying to find out.

"It was the ha and ho business that opened my eyes. Vivian used abbreviations and puns in her diary. It would have been fatuous to suppose that WW were initials. WWho. And then I saw it. Westward ho. But who is westward if not Eileen West? I lean west. That was the pun. Once I saw that, it was all over."

"Of course," Joyce said, making a face at Kim over the starched headdress of Sister Mary Teresa. "It's as plain as can be."

"Once it's been pointed out," Emtee Dempsey purred.

"That's what I meant."

"The last line ends with a symbol," Kim said. "What does it mean?"

"It often shows up when WWho does. Doubtless Eileen was her supplier. Can't you guess the meaning of the symbol?" The old nun's smile was full.

The symbol was < followed by a sprinkling of dots. Kim said she gave up.

"What did Vivian Hoy die of? A combination of liquor and drugs. Did you hear Richard mention coke to Wilma? Cocaine. And what is cocaine called by addicts?"

"Angel dust," Joyce cried, and she and Kim stared at the symbol.

Kim said, "For heaven's sake."

"Explain it," Joyce pleaded.

"< is an angle, the dots are dust."

And Joyce quite rightfully groaned. Kim turned to Sister Mary Teresa. "Now, will you please tell me what you were doing yesterday driving around Chicago with Mr. Rush?"

"Diverting the police so that Joyce could go to Belmont Harbor and ask Jason Smally and Wilma a few questions. She got the right answers and they agreed to sail from Belmont Harbor to our dock. Which they did."

"Were you *alone* in the car with Mr. Rush, Sister?"

Sister Mary Teresa pushed back from her desk and rose from her chair. Her cheeks were rosy as she pulled her watch from her bodice and made a reproving noise.

"Compline," she said. "It's past time for Compline."

And so what was left of the Order of Martha and Mary— Sisters Mary Teresa, Kimberly, and Joyce, an improbable trio, perhaps, but sisters in religion and friends besides—went down the hall to the chapel to say their night prayers.